Spinner's Inlet

Spinner's Inlet

BY

Don Hunter

Horsdal & Schubart

Horsdal & Schubart Publishers Ltd.
Box 1
Ganges, BC, V0S 1E0

Most of the stories in this book appeared in *The Province* newspaper, in Vancouver.

Cover painting and line drawings in the text by Patricia Brown, Ganges, BC.

Design and typesetting by The Typeworks, Vancouver, BC.
This book is set in Perpetua.
Printed and bound in Canada by Hignell Printing Limited, Winnipeg, Manitoba.

This book is for June, Susie and Taryn, and in loving memory of Mary and Syd Hunter.

Canadian Cataloguing in Publication Data
    Hunter, Don, 1937-
       Spinner's Inlet

       ISBN 0-920663-06-0

    Title.
    PS8565.U57S6 1989   C813'.54   C89-091004-9
    PR9199.3.H86S6 1989

Contents

The Beginning   1
Here Comes The Bride   4
Bare Buttocks and Blackberries   7
Trimming the Sinners   9
Going To The Dogs   12
Getting Rachel's Goat   14
A Saw-horse Standoff   16
Labour Day Pains   18
Two Hats From Heaven   21
Tee Time   23
The Tide Turns   26
Face to Face   28
Here Comes Santa   31
Inch By Inch   34
Memories   36
From the Top   38
A Suit For Svensen   41
Promises, Promises   43
Passport Predicament   46
Rachel's Visitor   48
And That's the Law   51
Lottie's Luck   54
A Witching Well   57
Home, Sweet Home   60
Partners   62
A Dog and Its Boy   65
Miss Weaver   68
Prices and Values   71

State of the Arts 74
Peace Walks 76
Sporting Spirit 78
A Warming Trend 80
Facts of Life 82
Brothers 85
The Expert Touch 87
The Right Spirit 90
Old Soldiers 92
Verse and Worse 94
Double Fault 98
Back in the Saddle 100
Out of Line 103
Arts and Craft 105
Two of a Kind 108
A Log of Love 110
Show Horse 112
Mr. Mayhem 114
Scratch and Sin 117
Lucy Holds the Fort 119
With a Little Help 121
One Day a Child Was Born 123
Blowin' in the Wind 127
Tub or Not Tub 130
Water Ways 133
Psychic Sidekicks 135
Smokin' 'em Out 138
The Vicar's Ferry Tale 140
Joe Flynn's Trucker 142
Smoothing the Route 148
Rocking the Boat 152
All of a Lather 156
Bargain Day 161

The Beginning

The two young Martin girls sat with their chins in their hands, frowning at Wilson Spinner.

"You mean they walked from Sidney, all the way into *Victoria?*" Jillian, at nine, two years older than her sister, was skeptical.

"Why didn't they catch a bus?" young Julie asked.

Wilson laughed. "They walked it—18 miles—*after* they had rowed from here to Sidney, and the rowing used to take them from breakfast to supper time! No ferries, no buses, no nothing." The girls were quiet as they considered such a state of affairs.

"What else does it say, Wilson?" Jillian indicated the heavy, leather-bound tome open on Wilson's knee. The book was the Spinner family journal, started by the patriarch, Samson Spinner.

In 1855, 26-year-old Samson had abandoned the bleak life of a collier in the mines of England's northwest county of Cumberland, where the narrow seams ran for miles out under the Solway Firth and men worked the coal-face with picks and shovels, on their knees, and often lying on their sides, in fetid water, for wages that barely kept a family fed. He and his 19-year-old bride, the former Maud Skillings, had made the arduous ocean-and-land journey to what later would become British Columbia, and were among the first non-Indian settlers on the Gulf Islands.

Wilson had read to the girls Samson's description of arriving with his young wife almost a century and a half ago. A small rowboat had been lowered from the merchant ship they had boarded in Victoria, and the young couple had climbed down into it. Their belongings, in two trunks, had been lowered after them. The following day, after a night camped on the 20 acres they had purchased from the Hudson's Bay Company for one pound an acre—money scrimped by two generations of two families of miners—they had rowed out again to claim the first of their livestock—one milk cow in calf, two oxen, a crate of chickens, and a yearling bay stallion. Everything except the chickens had been shoved, protesting, off the back of the boat, and encouraged to swim.

"Holy doodle!" said Julie.

Wilson read from the journal: "Regrettably, both of the oxen and the stallion at first chose the opposite shore as their destination. Only after considerable and repeated efforts were we able to persuade the beasts that their health and future well-being—to say nothing of our own—would be best served by them adjusting their bearings and making their way to the flat beaches of what soon we would name, Spinner's Inlet."

Jillian laughed. Julie looked a little puzzled. "The horse and the oxes thought they were supposed to go to Saltspring or somewhere," Jillian explained. "Old Samson and Maud chased them back here from their boat. Else goodness knows what might have happened."

Goodness knows, indeed, Wilson agreed. He had taken the journal down off its shelf after returning with the girls from a walk up Spinner's Mountain. From the top they had watched the grey-green silted edge of the Fraser's late spring freshet where it crept out into Georgia Strait and towards the bays and inlets of the outer Gulf Islands.

It was that sight that had prompted Wilson later to open the journal, while the three of them, with mugs of hot chocolate, sat in the sprawling Spinner home before the huge beach-stone fireplace built by the pioneers.

Wilson had read from the page filled with the firm, neat hand of Samson Spinner. Samson had remarked on the waters from the mountains at the head of the Fraser Valley that had spilled down into the great river and swelled it so that in its rush to the Pacific, it had taken with it large parts of the few small farms and much of the livestock of the settlers who had placed their future in the lush lands of its valley and delta.

He had described the scores of bloated pigs, stiff-legged cows, and whole flocks of drowned geese and ducks, floating past the Inlet, along with complete and partial barns and farm outbuildings.

The girls had sipped on their hot chocolate, imagining the scene.

"It must have been really something if the ducks drowned," Jillian observed. She came around behind Wilson and examined the journal and its even script.

"So Samson—the first Samson—was your—?"

"Great-grandfather," Wilson said.

Julie stared at him. "Well, he must have been *real* old," she said, "because you're old, aren't you?"

Wilson laughed. "I suppose I am."

Jillian said, "So where do we come in? We're not Spinners, exactly, are we?"

"Here." Wilson turned back the pages to the front, and the Spinner family tree. Jillian's brow crinkled as she read the names and tried to understand the connections.

Wilson took her finger and traced the route. "Your great-grandmother was Victoria Spinner, who was old Samson's granddaughter. Victoria married Henry Martin; they had a son, Douglas, and he had a son, Paul."

"My dad!" declared Julie.

"Right," Wilson agreed.

Jillian nodded. "I think I get it," she said.

A little later Wilson watched them heading off home, past the stand of massive cedars that had been tall when old Samson and Maud had arrived. Jillian tossed her blonde hair back and he heard her words on the wind.

"Can you believe that, them walking all that way? To Victoria? That is really awesome."

Wilson decided that old Samson would have enjoyed the thought. He looked down to the beach, to where Samson and Maud had finally steered their animals, and from where they must have studied the site that they would set aside for their home. He smelled woodsmoke from the chimney they had built of rocks from the beach, the scent mingling with that of the giant firs and cedars that stood back from the house. The Martin girls turned and gave a final wave before they rounded the curve in the driveway, and Wilson lifted a hand and watched them out of sight. Then he went back inside and replaced the journal on its shelf. He told himself, not for the first time, that Samson Spinner had made a pretty smart move.

Here Comes The Bride

The marriage of Evelyn Plummer to Jackson Spinner continued an Inlet tradition. It maintained the mingling of the native heritage with that of the first English settlers, keeping intact the blend of stoicism and eccentricity, and the ceremony was concluded despite most things going wrong that could.

The first time a young Spinner man married an Indian girl was back in the 1880s. She travelled by canoe from halfway down the island and the canoe started sinking as it approached the Spinners' family dock. The composure with which she stepped out, fully clothed, into the waist-deep water and made her way ashore vastly impressed the stiff-collared and parasoled English.

For Evelyn's marriage to Jackson the main transportation was by rented school bus, the consideration being that the fewer cars on the road after what would no doubt be a substantial celebration, the better. Given that admirable reasoning it was an oversight at best that Jackson's uncle, Nelson Spinner, was the designated driver. The bus was detailed first to meet the ferry bringing the mainland guests and then to travel along Ennerdale Road picking up local guests and wedding-party members, including the groom.

The *Gulf Queen* was even more behind schedule than usual. Nelson passed the time on the wharf with Svensen and a couple of loungers who joined with him in a pre-nuptial toast to the bride. And one to the groom. One to the bride's mother, to a honeymoon baby. . . . The bus was 30 minutes behind schedule when it lurched up the hill towards an agitated Jackson Spinner and his best man. It stopped; the motor chugged, sighed, and died.

"It's been doing that," observed Nelson, as he stepped carefully down and opened the hood on the second try.

There followed an extended period of grumbling and worse from under the yellow hood, as Nelson, armed with a wrench and screwdriver, failed to locate the problem and apparently repeatedly injured his knuckles. Finally, "Move over, Nels," said the only other mechanic on hand, and the bridegroom rolled up his sleeves.

At the Church in the Vale, the Reverend Randall Rawlings was frowning at Jackson's mother, Melinda, reminding her he had a christening to do as well, when the bus rolled up and Jackson Spinner stepped down to be wed.

He looked like the before-half of a detergent commercial where the smiling unharrassed mother gets all the grease and dirt out in one half-minute wash. Melinda whooped and started falling backwards at the sight of her son, streaked with motor oil from his handsome, tanned brow to his finger tips, by way of his shirt, tie, and buttonhole carnation. She flung out a hand for balance and smacked the just-arrived maid of honour, her daughter Joanne, below the left eye. Joanne yelped, and swore loudly.

Jackson's father, Dixon, made a brave attempt to clean up his son, using the age-old spit-on-the-hankie-and-rub method. It worked the oil and dirt into a pancake makeup that spread from brow to chin and back to both ears, and stirred some droll observations about palefaces from the bridal group. Dixon quit wiping and stowed the filthy hankie back in the breast pocket of his new, dove-grey, three-piece suit.

Joanne's yelp had inspired a matching cry from Nelson Spinner's beagle, Brandy, who was confined to the bus. But whereas Joanne's cries subsided, Brandy's continued, and increased in volume.

The Reverend Rawlings was fast running short of that peculiar understanding required when dealing with island events. His schedule was off by 45 minutes, and there was no sign of the bride.

He was about to suggest to Melinda that the wedding be called again for the following week, when Evelyn arrived, chauffeured by her father, Chief Jimmy Plummer. She was a picture-book princess, her startlingly white gown touched here and there with brilliant and intricate beadwork, courtesy of her cousin Sheila Charlebois from up around Fort Nelson. Evelyn studied the scene, smiled, and went to Melinda and clasped her hands.

"I checked on the ferry and waited a bit longer," she said.

She barely blinked at the sight of Jackson, now being ushered out of her way, and she took the Reverend Randall Rawlings gently by the arm and patted his sleeve.

"A little late, but everything will be just fine now," she said.

And it was.

Evelyn fixed her eyes on Rawlings and held his gaze while the ceremony was accompanied by the relentless baying of the bus-bound Brandy. She assisted Jackson when he fumbled the ring and she giggled and wiped an oil smudge from his nose before she kissed him.

The Reverend Rawlings wished them both well as they signed the register and then, while the wedding pictures were being taken, he walked alongside the bus and addressed the beagle in some decidedly un-Christian-like terms.

Bare Buttocks and Blackberries

The radio personality likely will remember last summer for the day he went skinny dipping on the Brigadier's beach. The Brigadier was out shooting trees when it happened. It was Mrs. Brigadier who saw him first. She was sitting on the sun-deck sipping tea and viewing Vancouver's hazy outline with a disapproving eye. She straightened up when the radio man, whom she had seen heading for the water, dropped his pants, and, "Simon!" she called.

The Brigadier was around the point and at her yell he came striding, six-feet-four, straight as a Douglas fir, and his old .303 Lee Enfield held in a somewhat questing position. He had just shot the top ten feet off a presumptuous balsam that was threatening his view across the gulf to the rest of Canada. He had used 17 rounds; not one of his better days.

"What's that, m'dear?" he called, and Mrs. Brigadier pointed.

Bare chubby buttocks, framed and inflated by bands of summer sunburn above and below. The radio personality turned at that point full face to the Brigadiers.

"Good gracious!" said Mrs. Brigadier.

The last time the Brigadier had heard the radio man, who does one of those open-mouth programs on the mainland, the man had been ranting about police excesses and had gone on to criticize the "rigid and dangerous military mentality" that he saw asserting itself on the rights of Canadians. The Brigadier had whacked the radio with his cane and it had not sounded well since then.

Subsequently the Brigadier had not joined in the polite cooing that arose when *The Tidal Times* social page reported that the radio personality had bought the Dutchman's place and from now on would be on view in and around the Inlet.

"Damned cheek!" the Brigadier snorted as he marched across the sandstone slabs towards the naked hotliner.

"What the hell do you think you're doing?" he demanded.

Give the fellow his due. He faced right up, put his pudgy hands firmly on his hips and said, "Going swimming, of course."

"Like that?" The Brigadier pointed with his cane while looking the man straight in the eye.

The radio personality nodded but his hands drifted down from his sides. "There's no law that says I must be covered," he said. "It's a matter of individual rights, a matter of the democratic principle, as I constantly remind my listeners."

The Brigadier, who with four rows of ribbons leads the Legion parade every Remembrance Day, flinched as the man invoked democracy. He had acquired the ribbons, and a couple of battlefield promotions, partly through a shrewd grasp of strategy. He nodded, turned about and marched smartly toward the sun-deck.

Mrs. Brigadier quickly rearranged the drapes and called to him from the sitting room. "Did you send him off?"

"Not yet," said the Brigadier, lifting the phone.

The radio personality left the ocean feeling refreshed and reasonably smug, until he realized his clothes had gone from the log where he'd left them. The sun had dipped behind the spine of the island, and it was chilly. The tide had moved in swiftly as he swam, leaving only the dirt road that flanked the Brigadiers' house as an exit. Through that, though, and it was just a short dash to his car. There were no lights at the Brigadiers.

He stepped onto the dirt road and was just under the first post of the sun-deck when the floodlight went on and offered the seven members of the Spinner's Inlet Ornithological Society an unarrested view of what the Brigadier had promised them would be "a rare specimen indeed, m'dear." The radio personality was accelerating even as the seven sets of binoculars were trained on him and was gone before Miss Bell-Atkinson, who had dropped her glasses, could refocus. There was reason to believe he made considerable contact with the Brigadier's blackberry patch on the way out. The ladies pretended they heard nothing.

For the rest of the summer the radio personality became very busy fixing up the yard and was seen but rarely. And for weeks the Brigadier surprised acquaintances by suddenly uttering little snickers of laughter for no apparent reason.

Trimming the Sinners

The bikers seemed to mean business from the minute the *Gulf Queen* docked and the seven of them came roaring and snorting off the car deck, throttles open and whooping like banshees as they thundered up the wharf. News of their arrival had preceded them. The skipper had phoned Sebastian at the ticket booth and he passed the word around the dock.

"Satan's Sinners, they are," Sebastian said.

Great timing, too. The young Mountie had been med- evacked to

Victoria the night before, where they'd nipped his appendix out. Not that anyone would have fancied the Mountie's chances against the seven, if it had come to that. They were a bad-looking lot. Big, and dirty, with grinning gap-toothed skulls and blood-dripping knives stencilled all over their helmets.

There've been bikers in Spinner's Inlet before, of course, and the odd dust-up with them. But never so many at one time, and so clearly hunting for trouble. They stopped at the top of the wharf, gunned their motors and milled around for a minute, then thundered away to the left, headed for the south end.

Reports on their progress between then and noon are sketchy. They did stop at the Cedars and put back five or six beer, and said they'd be back for more. As it turned out, they didn't show up.

About noon they had got down island as far as the Plummer house, where they stopped. Edward, the youngest of the three Plummer boys was in the yard painting a new sign for the Saturday-night dances at the community hall: "Dance Sat." When the bikers stopped, the other brothers stepped out onto the porch, James and John, the twins.

The bikers shouted across, asking if they had any beer, and when John shook his head, negative, two of them left their bikes and approached the snake rail fence. One of them said, "I never heard of a Indian shack with no beer, Chief," and his buddies hooted. Edward moved away from the sign and stepped up onto the porch, and the three brothers turned away and went inside and closed the plank door behind them.

One of the bikers tossed a rock at the door. Then another, and another. And they started yelling. All the tired old racist stuff, and some major threats. Then one of them jumped the fence. And that was when the Plummer boys came out again.

They were carrying chainsaws and they stopped just long enough on the porch to start them. Edward went for the one in the yard, who turned and ran face-first into the big hemlock, and went down. When he rolled over, the chain was flashing and snarling alongside his nose and that motor must have sounded like all the angels of hell coming just to carry him home. A dark patch spread on the front of his jeans. He screamed and closed his eyes and folded his arms tight across his stubbled chin.

John and James went after the main gang and there never was such raw screaming fear on a set of dirty faces as when the two young loggers advanced, the saws throbbing and growling like live things. Two of them fell off their bikes while trying to start them, another flipped his into the ditch and landed face down in a patch of brambles, and the other three lit out without a thought for their clubmates.

The Plummer boys went back and sat on the porch while the four who had had the worst of it crawled back onto their steeds and followed their buddies back up the highway. No one saw anything of them for the rest of the afternoon, but they certainly were a different set of sinners when they came down for the evening ferry to Tsawwassen.

The fellow who had met the hemlock was sporting two long, even rips down the front of his oily leather jacket, and he kept looking back up the wharf toward the highway.

There was a bigger than usual crowd there when the *Queen* berthed. In fact, the dock was full. The bikers were the first down the ramp and not one of them so much as lifted his head when Lennie Wilson, leaning over the rail as they passed, went "Varoooom! Varoooom!" in his best chainsaw imitation.

Going To The Dogs

The Spinner family enjoys nothing more than indulging in those traditions that most characterize the land of their beginnings. This time, Nelson Spinner organized a hound trail.

He'd seen the real thing in visits to Spinner cousins still sprinkled in villages along the Solway Plain and into the English Lake District: Upwards of 20 hounds, similar to but bigger than the foxhound, following a laid-down scent on a cross-country circuit for a dozen miles or more while bookmakers call the odds on each and a lot of money changes hands.

There were no actual hounds available for Nelson's trail, so he ruled eligible all dogs resident in Spinner's Inlet and any who were visiting on that particular Saturday. He made it known that for the sake of verisimilitude he would assume the role of bookie and would be accepting wagers on the race. For that he was dutifully reproached by the Reverend Randall Rawlings, who nevertheless added that if he were a betting man, Nelson's beagle, Brandy, at 25-1, would invite a five-dollar fling.

Nelson laid the trail himself, dragging behind him a burlap pad soaked in a heady mixture of aniseed and paraffin, said to be irresistible to any real trail hound. He cut the distance to a quarter of the real thing, a concession, he said, to any short, fat dogs that might fancy their chances. He also modified the traditional British starting signal of a dropped white hankie, choosing instead to have the Brigadier signal the "off" with his .303.

The start was in the field behind Svensen's place, and the Brigadier marshalled the lineup. "Tall dogs on the right, short ones on the left!" he commanded, and there was a flurry and some quite snappish debate about whether tall was to the shoulder or to the top of the head before the entrants were in approximate line, held by their owners.

Svensen's amiable German shepherd, Conrad, was toward the tall end. His ears pricked when the Brigadier bellowed, "Ready!" The gun boomed. Conrad left the ground vertically, legs stiff, landed, and began vigorously chasing his tail.

He stopped that when Miss Bell-Atkinson's basset hound, Sarah, a non-contestant, waddled past; in a remarkable show of purpose and dexterity, Conrad mounted her. Miss Bell-Atkinson screamed "Rape!" at the Swede. Sarah looked at first surprised, then quite pleased.

A visiting collie, a lean loper that Nelson had been laying with two others as even-money favourite, took an immediate liking to the Brigadier who, being opposed to overt displays of affection, smacked the dog smartly across the chops with his cane and ordered it to heel, where it went and sat, quivering, and resolutely ignoring Nelson's cry of, "Run, you stupid bastard!"

The rest of the pack got away, in a fashion, yelping and wailing toward the far fence, with Nelson running behind, shooing them like chickens. About two minutes into the race they hit the Derwent Kennels, run by Nelson's spinster sister, Rachel. She was vaguely aware of Nelson's hound trail, but not of its route, and her two setter bitches that were in heat were both out in the walking pens.

That nicely took care of the 18 contestants that were neither neutered nor female, and left three in the running. There was Brandy, a long, lolloping retriever-cross, and Lennie Wilson's old bull terrier, Windy, a beast of such girth it seemed to need viewing through a wide-angle lens. It was sucking air like an antique pump and was not long for the race.

The retriever-cross was a field in front of Brandy and increasing its lead when it suddenly shot off to the right, through the gate in the fence around Froelich's swimming pool, attracted by barbecuing meat smells. Froelich is a surly being at the best of times, and in just a few seconds the dog came out again, tossed bodily over the cedar boards and landing with a thud, a gasp, and a whimper, before lurching to its feet and staggering off into the bush.

Brandy trotted on, nose to the scent, and accelerated gently as she re-entered Svensen's field to some polite applause from a clutch of tourists and cries of "fix!" from those who had bet the retriever-cross. Nelson, who had taken in $100 in small bets, was ignored as he attempted to argue the unpredictability of mixed breeds. Ignored by all but the Reverend Rawlings that is.

"A good day for all of us, Nelson," he said in front of a knot of Inlet natives. "Brandy wins the hound trail, and the church charity wins $125. It was a five-dollar bet I placed, wasn't it?"

The listeners applauded, and one of them brought a dish of water for the panting Brandy.

Getting Rachel's Goat

Wilson Spinner hunkered down in the morning sun and watched the *Gulf Queen* make a slow, scudding turn toward the dock.

He squinted and finally found the shape of his sister, Rachel, in the gloom of the car deck. She had phoned from the mainland and instructed him to meet the ferry and help her with "an addition" to her Derwent Kennels. He stared earnestly, taking in the leash in her hands and the animal, vaguely visible, on the other end.

"Looks like a bloody goat," he snorted. "Rachel's getting senile, I think." And Sebastian in the ticket booth hooted at the image. He stopped laughing when the ramp went down and Rachel came off dragging a stocky billy goat with a curve of horns that promised nothing but trouble.

The goat, pleased to be back on land, took a dead run at Sebastian but was grabbed by a whooping Wilson and the pair of them wrestled it down and then got it caged in Wilson's pickup.

"It was a bargain," Rachel explained to her brother. "I got it for $30 and they drove it down to the terminal."

Wilson glanced in the rearview mirror at the pair of yellow eyes framed in the cab window and thought, "I'll bet they bloody did."

"Why?" he said patiently. He had always considered Rachel his baby sister. The fact that she was now 63 didn't change a thing.

The kennel lawns, Rachel said. No more power mowers; they broke down, and the noise bothered her finicky pure-bred stock. The goat would mow the lawns from now on. Wilson helped her stake the beast, saw it had a good run of rope, and left.

Rachel answered the phone to Lennie Wilson's youngest boy, Charlie. She had promised him a choice from a setter litter in exchange for some odd-jobbing and cleanup.

"Come by tomorrow, Charlie," she said.

She went out just as the goat was starting on the third rose bush, having stripped two to the earth. On its way to the roses it had stopped long enough to sample Rachel's best linen bedsheets, hanging out to dry. A large corner of one was hanging, shredded. The grass all around was untouched, save for some chunky divots unearthed where the billy had pawed while winding up. Rachel yelled—a piercing, warlike shout.

The goat jumped and ran and the stake popped out of the earth. A spaniel bitch saw the horns and eyes coming for her, screamed and climbed halfway up the wire-mesh fence, fell down and ran yelping for cover. Svensen's German shepherd, Conrad, being boarded while the Swede vacationed, bared his teeth behind the wire and gave an unconvincing snarl. The billy goat lowered its head, charged, hit the mesh and knocked Conrad senseless and halfway across the kennels.

Rachel grabbed the end of the tether rope and managed to throw a couple of loops around a stump before she had to leave the lawn, with the goat just a short distance from her back end. She went inside and made a cup of tea. The goat wound the rope around the stump until it was halted, then started quietly nibbling at the grass. It was doing that when Wilson came by that evening, widening the grazed area evenly.

"So it's working, eh?" he said.

Rachel had taken in the washing and clipped back the ruined roses. She gave him an of-course-it's-working look.

"I'm not really sure that it's going to get along with the dogs, though," she said.

When young Charlie Wilson came around the next day, Rachel said, "Those pups are not quite ready, Charlie. A couple more weeks. But I've got a present for you meanwhile. You can tell your dad he'll never have to cut the lawns again."

A Saw-horse Standoff

When Sebastian Whittle and Charlie Logan fell out, things got nasty around Spinner's Inlet. The Whittles and the Logans are from early pioneer families. Charlie owns the Inlet store. Sebastian works for the ferries but, that not being a fulltime job, he also puts his hand to some carpentry.

Charlie had accepted Sebastian's quote for a modest extension on the store and everything had gone well until after the job was finished and Charlie noticed that the two excellent saw-horses were missing. He mentioned it to Sebastian.

"Well, they're mine," Sebastian said.

"They're not," said Charlie, "I watched you making them on time that I was paying for, from lumber that I bought."

Sebastian bridled. "It's a tradition, man," he said. "It's common practice—a carpenter makes the saw-horses he needs and takes them with him."

"Well, you must have a bloody barnfull by now," Charlie snapped.

"Anyway, those two are mine and I want them back. Two days," he added.

The saw-horses were not returned, and the cold war started. It was no different from politics or union contracts, where egos grab command, somebody says just the wrong thing, an ultimatum is tossed out and the challenge angrily grabbed. Both sides are painted into a corner and neither one will take the first step out, for fear of losing face.

The Whittles stopped shopping at the store, choosing instead to make extra trips to Victoria that must have been a thorough pain. And whenever the Logans came off the ferry, they looked through Sebastian as if he did not exist. It didn't stop there, of course. The Logan and Whittle blood-ties from marriages down through the years were severely strained.

The battle of the saw-horses became a community issue. People chose sides, and the ethics of the hired-man relationship were never so thoroughly examined. It likely still would have been going on if it hadn't been for the cloudburst the weekend that Sebastian and Marion were away overnight.

The water gushed down the hill behind the Whittles' house, spread swiftly across and filled the alder swamp at the back, then found a narrow channel and deepened it and started pouring down past the garden and in under the basement door.

Charlie Logan saw the flood as he was driving by. The water that the basement couldn't accommodate was racing around the side of the house and tumbling and frothing down the driveway, threatening to wash it out.

Charlie jumped from the car and raced up the drive. He broke open Sebastian's garden shed, grabbed a mattock and a shovel, and started digging a diversion. It's rocky around the Whittles' house, and the mattock bounced repeatedly, jarring Charlie's arm to the topmost bones.

It took him 40 minutes of non-stop slogging before he smacked out the last chunk of rock and earth and the stream of foaming water rushed into its new path, away from the house. Charlie's hands were bleeding and he was shaking when he finally leaned against the shed. He drove home and sank into a hot bath, holding a heavy straight Scotch.

Sebastian and his family arrived home, surveyed the damage, and saw the new trench. A community grapevine is a medium with a way of its own. That evening Sebastian knocked on the Logans' back door.

"It's not Christmas, " he said, when Charlie opened the door, "but. . . . " He pointed to the porch and two superbly crafted sawhorses made from two-by-six yellow cedar and three-quarter-inch plywood.

On one was written, "Peace", on the other, "Good will."

Labour Day Pains

Miss Bell-Atkinson had another testing day on the weekend. It was the 49th Annual Spinner's Inlet Labour Day Weekend Carnival and once again she had the feeling that there were those who did not wholly appreciate the contribution she made as Carnival Chairman, a title she had borne proudly—and in recent years defiantly—for three decades.

First, she swore that Wilson Spinner had, while participating in the pitch-and-putt contest, deliberately smacked a ball at Sarah, her slow-moving basset, causing the dog to sink the rest of the way to the ground and to lie shell-shocked for several minutes.

Wilson called as his defence several fellow golfers who testified that he could not, by design, hit a ten-acre field from across the road.

Miss Bell-Atkinson suggested there were some branches of the otherwise worthy Spinner family that could have been pruned.

She included Wilson's brother, Nelson, who she said had laughed at the prostrate Sarah from his post at the Crown and Anchor stall. And that Nelson should be linked in any way with a celebration of labour, she added, was a smack in the face to the working man or woman.

That was remarked on by some observers as being in poor taste; not because it wasn't necessarily true, but because it wasn't relevant to the issue.

Miss Bell-Atkinson stalked away, muttering about "no thanks . . . ought to do the blasted job themselves . . . " and walked into the middle of a rising dispute between Svensen and Chief Jimmy Plummer.

The Swede had spent two hours in the wine and beer garden, chasing each vintage with the other, before aiming himself at the Chief's five-dollar-a-plate salmon barbecue where he paid, examined the dish, declared the barbecue a primitive thing, said the only good fish was a pickled fish, and announced that Swedes are the Chosen People.

Chief Jimmy responded. He suggested several creative things that the Swede might want to do with a pickled fish, pointed out that Svensen could find a lot of company in Stockholm, to where there are scheduled flights, stuck the five-dollar bill in the Swede's pocket, and retrieved the plate. Svensen was challenging Chief Jimmy to stand up and fight as Miss Bell-Atkinson appeared.

"Don't be a nuisance, Mr. Svensen," she ordered. "Eat something." She took the five-dollar bill and handed it to the Chief, who gave back the plate.

Svensen told her it was a bloody half-baked Carnival Chairman who could arrange nothing better than burnt fishes for the hungry. The Chief said performances such as Svensen's discouraged legitimate visitors, and he suggested the Carnival Chairman might do something about it for next year. She nodded slowly, her gaze aimed off into the distance.

She focussed, as he approached, on Elliott Smalley, owner, publisher, editor, chief reporter and photographer of *The Tidal Times*. They had long feuded over her refusal to be re-titled Chairperson. The committee this year had responded to Elliott's repeated harping about the carnival becoming "predictable," by importing a tea-cup reader, Madame Carlotta, and her tent, from Victoria. Elliott had just come from the tent.

"Well, it's something I suppose," he said. "Same old rubbish, mind you. She told me to watch my step in the near future." He snickered and walked off, clutching his notebook and camera.

A voice rose above the general rumble of the crowd. It came from a large, florid-faced, disgruntled-looking man, obviously a tourist.

"All the way on the damned ferry for this?" he complained to his woman companion. "Wasps all over the goddamn salmon, warm beer, and a pile of bloody junk for sale."

He was opposite Lennie Wilson's "Pre-Owned Items" stall and, admittedly, it was not an inviting sight. Lennie wore a change apron and was shouting, "Lawnmowersbedspringsandotherlovelystufforsale! My price or yours!" Many of the items were rusty and several were veterans of more than one Carnival. They spent the winters in Lennie's workshop.

"You have to wonder why they bother," the tourist sneered.

Which was just about what Miss Bell-Atkinson was thinking again. She had on several earlier occasions been tempted to resign and leave them all to it.

"This time I really shall," she confided to Sarah as they left for the parking area. She was getting into her car when a siren started whooping and she saw the ambulance picking a path through the crowd. She hurried over, and Chief Jimmy turned around.

"Nothing serious," he said. "Elliott was trying to talk and walk at the same time and fell over one of Lennie's lawnmowers. He may have cracked a couple of ribs."

Miss Bell-Atkinson said that was really too bad, and she headed off for her car.

"Well, I'm definitely going to at least *consider* resigning," she said, patting Sarah's head.

Two Hats From Heaven

Patrick Shannon was somehow always on hand when the Martin girls ran into trouble. He had stopped at the Martin home for coffee the morning when Julie, the youngest, fell down the basement stairs.

She tripped at the top, yelled, then bounced off every one of the 14 steps before flipping over and hitting the cement floor with her forehead. She was silent for two seconds, then her wind came back and she started up.

Patrick was down the stairs in a flash, belying his huge frame and his 68 years, and had her cuddled up in his bearish arms and comforted before anyone else had moved.

He put butter on her bump, spreading it softly with a great, splayed forefinger that bore the marks of 50 years of labouring from Alaska to Mexico, and which had supervised the trigger of a Bren gun at the battle of Dieppe.

He fished in his pocket as the youngster's cries subsided, and brought out a tiny mock-soapstone carving of an Inuit hunter. It was threaded on a shoelace and he strung it round her neck and tied it. That settled her.

Patrick finished his coffee and was leaving when she said, "Did you bring the hats, Patrick?"

He snapped his fingers, exasperated. "Forgot 'em again," he said.

"Next week, for sure." He had promised both girls a tractor-company hat, like the one he always wore.

A week later he was there for his coffee again, when one of the kittens started choking and the kids started screaming. Patrick grabbed the kitten, squeezed its mouth open and, neat as you'd like, picked out a sliver of bone lodged across the back teeth. The kitten sneezed, and the girls laughed out their relief and awarded Patrick a large hug and damp kisses as he started to leave.

"I forgot the blasted hats again," he said.

The following week the Martins just saw him briefly. He was walking slowly along the bottom road and they stopped the car to chat. He said he'd been having trouble with a cough, and he was pale. He managed a chuckle when the older girl, Jillian, asked about the hats, and he said, "I'll remember next week for sure."

The Martins learned two days later that he'd been seeing a specialist in Vancouver, and that he did not have a long time left. That was early summer.

He stopped by the next week for coffee and said he was feeling a lot better with the treatment. The girls sat quietly with him and no one mentioned the hats. The Martins went away for three weeks at the end of July, and the first thing they did when they got back was to phone and ask about Patrick.

"He's gone," said Molly, his eldest daughter. "It was quick and he went peacefully and without much pain. We're having the wake at Wilson's place the day after tomorrow."

Wilson Spinner and Patrick Shannon had been lifelong friends and comrades. They had gone off to war together and had come back unscathed together from the Dieppe maelstrom.

Sheila Martin told the girls, and little Julie said, "Why does people have to die?"

All of Spinner's Inlet went to the wake. A lot of excellent liquor was taken, and each glass was raised to the large colour photo of Patrick taped to the wall above the punch bowl. The girls played around and joined in the Irish songs that the early Shannons had brought with them a hundred years before and which broke out in mid-afternoon.

The Martins were leaving when Patrick's wife, Beth, called them. She took the girls by the hand to the Shannon house next door, into the kitchen and up to the counter, where sat two tractor-company hats, each a bit worn.

"Patrick said to tell you he didn't forget," she said.

Sometimes they wear the hats to bed.

Tee Time

The Spinner's Inlet Golf Links and Country Club was finally opened with some fanfare and an invitational tournament. The first-string sports columnist from the Vancouver morning paper described it as one of the more arresting experiences of his considerable career.

The Brigadier had been seething ever since Dixon Spinner was elected club president. The executive had considered the possibility of a confrontation marring the opening, and had decided that the way to appeasement lay in placing the responsibility for the brass band and the music cues in the Brigadier's hands. They apparently misjudged.

Afterwards, the Brigadier maintained the bandmaster simply had anticipated his signal. In any case, just as Dixon reached the top of his inaugural backswing, the bandmaster dipped his baton and the opening bars of "Colonel Bogey" crashed out from 23 assorted horns and drums. Dixon came unfastened and the ball rocketed out to the left and skidded out of bounds. The spontaneous applause was withheld, except by the Brigadier, whose large hands went at it like a pair of paddles.

It was agreed that Dixon should take a Mulligan and his second shot climbed high and straight. The band struck up again and the course was officially open.

Things were going well until the golf balls started disappearing in the fourth-hole woods bordering the parking lot. In the first foursome, the Reverend Randall Rawlings and Dixon each lost a ball. In the second, all the balls went missing.

It was Miss Bell-Atkinson who caught a glimpse of Nelson Spinner's beagle, Brandy, with a day-glow-orange golf ball startlingly visible between her jaws. She followed the dog at a trot through the woods, right to Nelson's pickup, where Brandy deposited the ball carefully beside five others resting against a rear wheel.

Nelson, in a foursome with Lennie Wilson, the Vancouver columnist, and Elliott Smalley, editor of *The Tidal Times*, told Miss Bell-Atkinson that Brandy had always fancied being a retriever, and that dogs will be dogs. He patted the beagle and whispered, "*Under* the truck, dummy."

By the middle of the afternoon the groups were strung out along the course. Back at the club, young Charlie Wilson was cleaning up the equipment shed. He straightened up and accidentally leaned on the switch that operates the club's just-installed and much-discussed sprinkler system. He snapped it off immediately, but the damage was done.

Miss Bell-Atkinson was lining up a five-iron shot. She stiffened and slowly raised her head and shoulders as the sprinkler head arose between her feet and the water fountained straight up. No one spoke.

Miss Bell-Atkinson adjusted her stance, swung, and said, "Good show!" as she dropped the ball on the green, pin-high. The Reverend Randall Rawlings turned to Dixon Spinner: "It didn't dampen her enthusiasm, anyway," he said.

Elliott Smalley, playing with the visiting columnist, was happy. Elliott was still recovering from rib damage sustained at the Labour Day weekend carnival but he was a trouper, as he explained to his colleague-in-print.

They were on the raised seventh tee and Elliott was advising that a nine iron was just right. Elliott swung and missed the ball. The columnist said nothing. Elliott swung harder, fell forward off the tee and started rolling down the hill, tiny grunts of pain emerging from his pursed lips.

"Let him be," Nelson said as the columnist made a move. "He should have played a wedge." People came and escorted Elliott back to the clubhouse.

Twice during the afternoon the columnist had noticed a tall man in black slacks, white shirt and peaked cap, cantering along the fairway, carrying a slim bag of clubs.

Now he came puffing up to the threesome, said " 'Scuse me," teed up, sliced a ball into the woods, and galloped after it.

"Sebastian," Nelson explained to the columnist. "From the ferry booth. If he ain't there on time the *Gulf Queen* will go right on by, again."

Some problems developed with the small lake at the eighth, after which Nelson insisted on giving the columnist three brand-new golf balls.

"I've got lots," Nelson assured him.

They came off the ninth green and Rachel Spinner directed them to a white-linen-clad table dressed up with a silver service.

"Tea?" she suggested.

Nelson snorted, but a glance from his older sister shut him up. He drifted away and selected a bottle of brandy from the complimentary bar. No one so far had chosen Rachel's tea.

She looked at the columnist.

"Lemon, please," he said, and Rachel knew that chivalry was not dead. The columnist took the bone-china cup, along with a cheese scone, and strolled over to Nelson and Lennie.

"In here," he said, and Lennie tipped the bottle. The columnist sipped, sighed, and sat down.

"I think I'll pass on the back nine," he said.

The Tide Turns

Sheila Martin was introducing the theme of "Conflict: Man Against the Elements" to her English class. "Take Mr. Spinner and Mr. Svensen and the cedar log," she said.

Wilson Spinner and his crony the Swede had liberated the log from some beach north of the Inlet and towed it as far as Svensen's before a falling tide hung it up. It was one of nature's better works; four feet through the butt, and straight as a pencil. Wilson envisioned a new roof of split-shake splendour for the old Spinner home. They bucked it into bolts and looped them with dog-lines. When the tide came in the bolts floated off in a very neat raft.

Wilson snagged the line to the back of his aluminum runabout and set out for his beach around the Long Point. Wilson, who's closing on 70, is occasionally surprised by events around him. In this instance it was the coughing of his motor as the gas ran out. He was in a flood tide and it was starting to run fast.

"I started drifting, kind of," Wilson recalled later.

Svensen watched intently from the shore as the waves, now bigger, and joining in dance with a sudden breeze, climbed up and around the little boat. First a cedar bolt would ride up on the swell, then Wilson; and another cedar bolt, then Wilson again.

"Like one of them horses on the carousel," the Swede said.

Wilson, still with the raft in tow, was paddling determinedly toward shore, using a piece of splintered plank, the closest thing on board to an oar. He was losing ground, and the sea was rising.

"I could only see that dirty grey toque of his finally," the Swede said, "up and down among the bolts and headed to sea."

The Swede cupped his hands and yelled, "Cut them loose, you dumb bugger!"

But Wilson bore down, dug at the ocean with the board, and did not advance. Svensen kicked the beach angrily, swore, then pushed off in his own dinghy and its six-horse kicker, which was just a little more useful than Wilson's paddle, given the state of the ocean.

A modest audience had gathered on the point by this time and they punctuated the ensuing chase with suitable commentary as the Swede closed in, yelling at Wilson, and Wilson cursed deeply as the cedar bolts waltzed around him and occasionally banged against his by-now bruised and frigid fingers.

The Swede slid into a trough, swooping broadside into Wilson's boat, and grabbed the gunwale.

"Let them go, Spinner!" he yelled. "They ain't worth it!"

"Bollocks," replied Wilson, and flailed with his board. But his determination was flagging and, as the wind rose, flicking foam now from the crests, he nodded to the Swede and, calling on one of the English colloquialisms retained by generations of Spinners, shouted, "Svensen, I'm knackered."

He waved a blue-grey hand at the bolts, now dancing defiantly around both boats. "They can go to frigging Boundary Bay if they want!"

Svensen sawed through a couple of the lines and slowly towed half a dozen bolts and Wilson to the Spinner beach. There they turned and watched the rest of the released raft dipping and dancing on the running tide until the swells took it from sight. There was polite applause when the pair wobbled up the beach, then hot rums and discussion about the basic treachery of a wind-assisted flood tide.

Wilson retired early and slept reasonably well, shouting out only twice in the night according to Barbara, his wife of 45 years. She called him about eight o'clock.

"Looks like the tide turned," she said.

Wilson stared down at the beach in the Inlet. The fugitive bolts, all in a row in the sun-speckled waters, bobbed gently in toward the beach. Wilson looked down at his swollen fingers and grunted.

"Man against the elements," Sheila said to the class. "Sometimes it's hard to pick a winner."

Face to Face

In the six months since he took over his uncle Sandy's veterinary practice, Scott McConville reckoned he'd got the people in Spinner's Inlet pretty well figured out. After the Hallowe'en costume ball, he's not so sure.

"Everybody goes," Joanne Spinner, daughter of Dixon and Melinda, told him. "Something to do with Celtic roots and Druid blood lines." He asked if he should pick her up but she just grinned and said no, she'd see him there.

Scott hunted up his old rugby jersey and socks, made up a horse-hair pigtail, and went as a matelot. He was the only one in the Legion Hall not wearing a mask. And the masks, and the fantastic costumes beneath them, erased identities.

He did manage to spot Sebastian fairly quickly. While the lanky ferry-booth operator was well done out in a guardsman's uniform, complete with busby, and hidden behind a bear-face mask, he was, as usual, flicking back his sleeve every few minutes to check the time and cocking his head in anticipation of the three blasts announcing the *Gulf Queen's* arrival.

Scott turned his attention to the bar, tended by Marie Antoinette. A Brian Mulroney was there, sporting a rubber mask with a chin like a front-end loader and the smile of a Kingsway car salesman. Beside him was a hyper John Turner, made-up face breaking into a manic grin, and clearing his throat every five seconds. The two of them ordered double ryes. Then they turned, and each raised slowly a single finger salute. Nelson Spinner and Lennie Wilson, Scott decided.

He worked his way to the bar and Marie Antoinette turned a long look on him. Joanne? Could be, he thought, right height. . . . At that point the French queen leaned forward to get a beer glass and gave Scott an uncluttered view down the front of her low-cut dress. It was not Joanne.

Florence Nightingale caught his attention. Twice she had been to the bar, twice ordered straight fruit juice. Joanne had been off liquor lately. She caught him watching her, nodded graciously, and moved off to the buffet. Scott moved after her but was waylaid by the Three terribly unsteady Musketeers.

They asked him, in hollow voices that rang suspiciously of Chief Jimmy Plummer's twin sons John and James, and their brother-in-law Jackson Spinner, for his professional confirmation of their opinion that the most-appropriate-costume award should go hands-down to Froelich, who was behind his wife in a two-person horse suit.

Florence, her Crimean robes enveloping her like a small tent, was now sitting next to Humphrey Bogart. She rose, and walked away as Scott approached. Bogey stood as well, then collected his camera and notebook from under the chair. No one had ever accused Elliott Smalley of being subtle in his years of running *The Tidal Times*.

The music had started again and the Lady with the Lamp was engaged in a slow waltz with a Shaman of the Coast Salish. The lights dimmed and Scott kept his eyes on the pair. They stayed at arm's length as they danced—one-two-three, one-two-three—which suited Scott. But he didn't understand why Joanne was being so coy. Over the last little while they had pretty well reached an understanding. The waltz ended and he headed for Florence, who saw him approaching and quickly walked away.

"Well, Jeezers!" he whispered, and went after her, cornering her near the coat rack.

"Hey there, lady, how much longer. . . . "

Florence snapped her mask off, and Rachel Spinner glared out from under the nurse's cap.

"Doctor McConville," breathed Joanne's spinster aunt and owner of the Derwent Kennels. "I know the Kennels' account is a week overdue. But I don't think the Hallowe'en ball is the place to pursue the matter. You've been trailing me all night, for heaven's sake!" She snapped her mask back on and whisked away. Scott waited for the floor to open and claim him.

Instead, a voice at his shoulder said, "Buy you a drink sailor?" Cleopatra stood there. Her face was heavily veiled. The rest of her was indisputably Joanne.

"I washed my hair," she said. "The dryer blew up on me. I'm late."

A large yellow pumpkin danced past them, engaged with a stern-faced Napoleon in a very slick fox-trot.

"You may, indeed," Scott said, turning to watch the twosome glide by. "And you can make it a double."

Here Comes Santa

"There are some kids in my class," said young Julie Martin, "who say there isn't a Santa Claus."

Paul Martin made a non-committal grunt and went back to sorting out the tangle of Christmas lights to string along the sun-deck rail.

"They say there isn't an Easter Bunny, either," the youngster continued. "Or even a Tooth Fairy for heaven's sake!"

Her dad bent low and dug deep in the box for an elusive bulb that seemed to take him ages to find. It was just the night before that they had slipped $1.06 under her pillow in an envelope with a note from the Tooth Fairy apologizing for being a day late with payment for a departed incisor.

"There were teeth falling out all over the place yesterday," the note had said. "Sorry. Have a lovely day. The Tooth Fairy."

And on her bedroom wall she still has the piece of paper with the muddy footprints of the actual Easter Bunny from last spring in plain and petrified sight.

"So what do you think? Is there really a Santa, Daddy?"

The older girl, Jillian, grinned at her father, then became interested in something midway between the front window and the horizon. The girls' mother, Sheila, had left the room as the query was put, and could be heard vigorously emptying the dishwasher in the kitchen.

"So what do you think, huh?"

Paul Martin sat back on his heels, examining the braids, the white teeth and the spaces, the little wrinkle on the bridge of the nose, and the soft hazel eyes. She had clung to it all far beyond the point at which her sister had caved in, but, he decided, she was going to have to face it sooner or later, anyway.

"Well, in fact love. . . . "

"Colette Levesque saw him last Christmas, you know," the youngster interrupted. "She even talked to him."

Three weeks before last Christmas, Henri Levesque had been nailed by a falling snag while clearing more of their ten-acre stump ranch at the bottom end of the island, and fractured his hip. Marie went into labour at the news, and the young transplanted Quebec couple wondered suddenly what had hit them. There was no unemployment insurance or workers'compensation for Henri, who disdains any form of state support and whose payment to Dr. Timothy for two previous deliveries had been in chickens, regardless of Dr. Timothy's preference.

Henri and Marie's middle one, Colette, subsequently described to the Martin girls in breathless detail how Santa, in a pickup truck something like the kind Mr. Nelson Spinner drives, had swung quietly into the Levesque front yard just before midnight on Christmas Eve.

She said he spoke English, sort of, because, leaning out of her window, she heard him use some of the words she had heard Mr. Svensen use. This happened when the Levesques' border collie, Marcel, took a militant run at the unfamiliar red suit. Colette raced downstairs to the rescue, only to find Marcel happily licking the old man's hand, wriggling his bum and conducting the meeting with his tail.

"And you know what Marcel is like with strangers, unless they're kinda magic, like him," Julie counselled as she recounted Colette's story. Paul Martin said indeed he did.

The old gentleman at that point had made a "shush" sign to Colette and pulled his hood closer to his face, then hauled out two large sacks festooned with ribbons and sprigs of green and laid them on the porch.

"Colette asked him where the reindeers were," Julie said, "and he said he was very sorry to say that they had the flu."

Paul Martin nodded. "There was a lot of it around at the time," he agreed.

The contents of the sack, including one fairly fat envelope, set the Levesques up for Christmas and a bit beyond; Henri got back on his feet with the help of Dr. Timothy, and they haven't looked back since.

"So, we know there's an Easter Bunny," Julie concluded. "And we know there's a Tooth Fairy. And we know what happened to the Levesques. So what do you think, huh?"

Paul Martin thought that he had never seen his older girl so intensely absorbed in the view from the front window, nor had he ever known his wife so quiet in the kitchen. He fiddled around and finally got the errant bulb screwed into the socket.

Then he looked up at his youngest daughter, and the soft eyes. And he decided that, for now anyway, later was a much better idea than sooner.

"I think," he said, with a grin, "that if those kids from your class don't hang up their stockings, they're making a very big mistake."

Inch By Inch

The conversion to metric has been slow and not terribly successful in Spinner's Inlet. It's as though the whole community accepted Rachel Spinner's initial prediction that, "I don't think it will catch on around here."

The young Mountie has had his problems.

"I was doing 50," the Brigadier protested, jabbing at the speedometer on his Mini-minor.

"That's miles, sir," the constable said. "The road signs indicate kilometres."

"Bloody foreign rubbish," the Brigadier flared, snatching the ticket. "I've been to the continent, you know," he called, as the constable retreated. "Cheap plonk and snails, can't speak English, and most of the buggers don't take showers! Metric!" he snorted.

Rachel herself slammed the counter in Logan's store and rejected the dogfood bags labelled with kilograms.

"My dogs eat pounds," she declared.

Charlie Logan opened two of the big bags of dry meal and weighed the stuff out on his old scales.

"And I have miles to go, before I sleep," Rachel added as she strode out. "Tell Robert Frost about metric. The fools!"

The Reverend Randall Rawlings ran out of patience waiting for Sebastian to install a fan unit above the stove and decided to do it himself. He studied the diagrammed instructions and then, with the utmost care and a borrowed jigsaw, cut a perfect ten-inch circle through the v-joint yellow-cedar kitchen wall, on out and through the exterior siding. The diagram figures were in centimetres, and the hole was 2-1/2 times too big. It took a lot of patching and stuffing to fix it, and the outside's a ruin.

Lennie Wilson ran into trouble when he attempted to convert millimetres of pesticide to match the liquid-ounce level on his spray bottle. The lawns died within 48 hours, his gooseberry crop wilted, then dropped, and the billy goat that Rachel had given to young Charlie started walking in circles and had to be tied to a tree in the bush and fed by hand.

Froelich messed up measuring the chemicals for his swimming pool and for three weeks his wife hid in the house, afraid the rest of her hair would fall out and accusing Froelich of trying to put her away. Nelson Spinner said he would have thought that anyone with a name like Froelich would know all about foreign measures, and Froelich, whose father had been a sod-buster in Saskatchewan, said he would take Nelson to the Human Rights Branch if there were any more discriminatory remarks.

Miss Bell-Atkinson's mouth quivered when Scott McConville, the new vet, told her that Sarah's temperature was 38.6.

She stroked the old basset hound lovingly and said, "Is this good-bye, then?"

"No, it's quite normal," Scott said, withdrawing the Celsius thermometer and pointing to the conversion chart on the wall. Miss Bell-Atkinson hoisted Sarah and stomped out in a snit.

Elliott Smalley took the matter in hand and wrote a page-one editorial in *The Tidal Times* that chided the residents of Spinner's Inlet for their mulish reluctance to get in step with the rest of Canada, and their obvious lack of respect for the lawmakers of the land.

"Back up your elected representatives!" he exhorted.

That produced a picket line outside his office led by Wilson Spinner and the Swede, carrying signs that said: "You've put your .3048-metre in your mouth again, Smalley." And, "Al Jolson said it best: I'd walk 1,609,00 kilometres for one of your smiles, my m-a-a-ammy!" And, "Back up your MPs—against the wall!" Their point made, the pickets applauded each other warmly and waved indelicately toward Smalley's office.

"A beer, now, perhaps?" Wilson Spinner suggested.

The Brigadier nodded. "A pint," he said.

Memories

The back end of the year is always a bad time for Nelson Spinner. Too much time on his hands. Too many memories. From spring on he's busy planting and tending and then harvesting and marketing the produce that has been the Spinner family mainstay for almost a hundred years. After October, things are slow. . . .

Nelson trundled his pickup down to the marina and called in on young Jackson Spinner, his nephew.

"Buy y'a coffee," he said.

Jackson shook his head and waved at the stripped-down motor he was working on.

"Too busy, Nels. Next time, eh?" Nelson drove back down the highway and turned in at the Wilson place. Lennie would be home.

"Can't talk to you now, Nels. Maybe a beer later," Lennie said. "Maggie's laying the law down. Paint the bedroom or sleep in the yard." He grabbed a tray and a roller and went inside.

Nelson nursed the truck around the turns and swung into the driveway of the Derwent Kennels. His older sister Rachel was measuring food into the various dishes of her breeding and boarding canines. Nelson started to help but twice matched a dog with the wrong food. Finally Rachel said, "Go put the kettle on, Nels."

They sat over a cup of tea and Nelson would have lingered but Rachel cleared the cups. "Come on Nelson, I've work to do. I'm too busy for you now." She looked down at him. "You should have married again, you know."

Nelson drove away, and he thought again of Bronwen. It was 1947. Nelson had stayed on in the UK after his demob from the RCAF, searched out his Spinner roots in the far northwest county of Cumberland, and landed up in Wales. They were in a small, white-washed pub in the shadow of the bomb-scarred Llandaff Cathedral on Cardiff's northern skirts.

"Bronwen Williams," she had said, in the quiet song of the Rhondda Valley, and Nelson had known right then. They were married in a greystone chapel at the foot of a street of colliers' houses, and they honeymooned at Tenby, where they walked windswept beaches and later warmed themselves by a great coal fire.

On their last weekend before leaving Britain she took him to Cardiff Arms Park where Wales was playing its first international game since the end of the war. Nelson recalled in tingling detail the singing before the game and especially, with bare minutes to the kickoff, the sudden brief hush, and then the first two haunting notes of the Welshman's national song—"Mae Hen Wlad Fy Nhadau"—"Land of my Fathers"—and then the thousands of voices rising and soaring in harmony and travelling to the stunning climax, and being instantly replaced with a crashing, welcoming roar as the red-shirted rugby 15 trotted out onto the pitch.

The singing had sent a tear to Nelson's eyes and a shudder through his soul. "Passionate lot, you Welsh," he had said, and her dark eyes had laughed.

He brought her to Spinner's Inlet and their honeymoon didn't stop. Nelson's father, old Andrew, said he'd often wondered what kind of woman would tame his middle son, and now he knew.

Bronwen was pregnant soon after they arrived, and Nelson walked on air. "We'll call him David," he said. "For your saint fellow."

Bronwen went into labour two months prematurely, and hemorrhaged. Nelson held her hand and prayed. She and her son died before the mainland doctor arrived. They were buried side by side in the Spinner's Inlet cemetery where each spring a small stand of yellow daffodils marks their place.

Nelson brushed a hand across his face and slowed down for the curve past young Jackson's and Evelyn's house. He hadn't seen much of Evelyn since the couple's marriage in the summer. He was shifting into third when he saw Evelyn waving wildly at him from the front porch. He pulled into the driveway and stopped.

"Nels!" she called, laughing. "Thank heavens you came by—the damned washing machine is flooding me out!"

He cleaned some junk out of the outlet hose and the wash continued. "There you go," he said.

Evelyn gave him a hug. Her dark eyes laughed.

"I don't know what we'd ever do without you," she said. "I really don't."

Nelson looked down at her and smiled. "Oh, you'd manage, Ev," he said. "You'd manage."

From the Top

Miss Bell-Atkinson's twin nephews, the bespectacled Harvey and Henry, have been stepping up their visits to the Inlet recently, anxious to have their cabin finished. They're a bit odd by Inlet standards. Remote, sort of.

They're identical—short, slight and blonde—and they belong to Miss Bell-Atkinson's younger sister from North Vancouver. It's either Harvey who's the computer genius and Henry the chemist, or vice versa. Either would be comfortable in a white coat.

"Laboratory specimens," Nelson Spinner tagged them disgustedly after twice trying to start a conversation and generating just a little "hummmm" and two matching mechanical smiles. He dismissed them after that.

Miss Bell-Atkinson considered the twins' reluctance to gossip with the likes of Nelson proof of superior breeding and taste. In the late summer she presented the delighted pair with an acre adjoining her own immaculate waterfront property, and a set of plans for a two-bedroom cabin.

Their intent to build was, of course, mentioned in the items column of *The Tidal Times*, and that grated painfully within the Spinner family ranks. The acre was part of the original Spinner family property up to about ten years ago, when tight times and a cash emergency had forced Wilson Spinner to put it on the market. A trust company offered the asking price, and Wilson sold. The company had been representing Miss Bell-Atkinson. The Spinners knew then that any chance that they'd had of repurchasing the property had gone out the window.

The twins accepted a quote from Sebastian for the construction, but he warned them they'd need patience, that the job would have to fit in with his other projects and his part-time job at the ferry booth.

For the first two weekends he let them help, but after Harvey, or Henry, twice severed a saw-horse while trying to build forms, and the other one slipped astride a scaffold pipe and sat hunched, keening and clutching himself for 20 minutes, Sebastian dismissed them.

"I'll be the builder, gentlemen," he said.

After that they observed, and grew restless. They frowned while Sebastian, using the chewed stub of a carpenter's pencil, studiously worked out a lumber order on a scrap piece of plywood and Henry, or Harvey, slipped his hand into his pocket and played feverishly with his super micro-computerized calculator that does everything but walk the dog.

They shuddered in tandem every Friday night as Sebastian sat down in Miss Bell-Atkinson's kitchen, and squirmed as, with the same chewed pencil and working on the back of a cigarette packet, he detailed the number of hours on which days he'd devoted to the cabin and how much, at $15.75 an hour—cash—he was owed. He shook his head when they offered him the calculator. "Don't trust 'em," he said.

Their patience gave out when Sebastian advised them there'd be a three-week break before he could start on the roof.

"We'll do it," they declared. "And it will require precisely 8.745 squares of re-sawn shakes to do it," announced Harvey, or Henry, triumphantly waving the machine.

They were on the roof, chortling, when Nelson Spinner stopped below. He had been past three times during the morning, slowing down briefly each time, glancing up, then moving on. They had about half the south pitch covered.

Nelson leaned out of the pickup window and looked up. His eyes had a peculiar light. The twins' clinical reserve fled before a bursting pride as they sat back and reviewed their handiwork.

"How does it look from down there?" one of them called.

Nelson scanned the roof. "Very neat," he nodded. "Those shakes could almost have been programmed to lie that straight."

They nodded and grinned. Nelson studied the meticulously spaced rows of exposed nailheads the twins had left behind as they worked down the roof, slipping the thin end of each shake under the thick end and nailing through the thick end.

"Mind you," he said, "you'll need a lot of buckets inside when the rain comes. Most people I know start shaking a roof from the bottom."

A Suit For Svensen

Always at Christmas time young Charlie Wilson thinks about the tin whistle. He still has it in a drawer, and the ribbon with it, the crimson ribbon.

He was about five, and the whistle, all golden and shimmering, lay in the middle of the Christmas display in the big window at Charlie Logan's store. His little soul ached out loud for it and he had yelled while half the village, including Svensen getting his groceries, had watched and chuckled as Charlie's mother shot him out through the doorway while advising him that the next tune he heard would be one played on his backside.

The next evening at the annual Inlet children's Christmas party Charlie's eyes had shamed the evening star as he watched the tin whistle, dressed in a crimson bow and held in Santa's gnarled hand, coming out of the old man's bag. The boy had clutched the whistle and walked backwards, awed.

Half the population of Spinner's Inlet has gone through the Christmas party on Svensen's knee, most of them convinced his reindeer were just resting up in the woods.

Svensen appeared in the Inlet about a dozen years ago and set himself up as a recluse. He made it clear that a man who had hand-logged in the Charlottes and seen the inside of every bunkhouse and beer parlour from Dawson City to Boston Bar required "nothing from nobody."

Barbara Spinner remembered watching him as he paced the beach around the Long Point hour after hour, whittling bone-white drift-wood sticks into paper shavings that floated down and settled in his footprints in the sand. As the second winter of Svensen's residence came and he remained alone, Barbara advised her husband Wilson that he, Wilson, would no longer be doing Father Christmas.

"You're too sick," she said.

"Wilson's sick, Mr. Svensen," she told the Swede on the eve of the annual party. "We've got to have a Santa."

Svensen demurred, insisting there must be others. After some considerable negotiating, he agreed. The next day he appeared in the red-and-white suit, and the children grasped his enormous hands and whispered past his amazing beard. It's been that way ever since. Barbara reminds Svensen it's time for St. Nick, he grumbles, she persists. Svensen capitulates, collects the suit, and all the kids come home smiling.

This year Barbara was ill; a bad case of pneumonia. Before flaking out she delegated the party details—not all of them wisely. She gave the Santa chore to Miss Bell-Atkinson.

"Just call Mr. Svensen and tell him we'd be happy if he played Father Christmas again and the suit is down at the hall." She wondered as she drifted into a medicated sleep if Miss Bell-Atkinson would handle it well.

Miss Bell-Atkinson didn't. She told the Swede to pick up the Santa suit and, when he hesitated and said in his customary fashion, "Oh, I don't know if I'll do it this year," she, with her customary brusqueness, said, "Very well, we'll find someone else," and rattled the phone down.

"So that's it, isn't it?" Charlie heard his mother say on the phone to Barbara a few days later. "There's no point in us asking him now. God knows who she'll get. Probably one of those two specimens she calls nephews. Anyway, I told her I'd be at the hall at five o'clock so she could pick up the suit."

Charlie sat for a while, then went upstairs. He came down, climbed onto his bike, and rode around until he spotted the Swede's truck. When Svensen came out of the store Charlie was sitting on a pile of split alder, playing a delicate air on a fine-looking flute with a crimson ribbon tied around it. His fingers moved deftly and the music rose into the quiet afternoon. The Swede stopped.

"That's a fine sound, Charlie," he said.

Charlie took the flute from his mouth. "Glad you like it, Mr.

Svensen," he said. "I have an audition in Vancouver in the New Year." He was quiet for a moment. "I got a penny whistle once from Santa Claus." He grinned. "That kinda got me started."

The Swede nodded but said nothing.

"Mr. Svensen," Charlie said. "Miss Bell-Atkinson is going down to the hall at five o'clock to pick up that suit. I don't know who she's going to put it on, but whoever it is, it's not going to fit, if you see what I mean."

The Swede turned toward his truck.

"He prob'ly won't know a damned thing about penny whistles," Charlie said.

The Swede turned back.

Charlie checked his watch. "She is always right on time," he said. "We can beat her by a good ten minutes."

The Swede frowned, folded his arms, and studied Charlie. The corners of his eyes crinkled and he nodded two or three times slowly, then he gestured toward the truck.

"I think we will go for that suit, Charlie," he said. "A knowledge of penny whistles is very important."

Promises, Promises

Nelson Spinner lit a cigarette, inhaled and blew out a smoke plume. Lennie Wilson watched him.

Finally, "Gimme one," Lennie said, and reached out his good hand. They were at the Spinner family annual New Year's Day lamb and salmon barbecue.

The night before, Lennie had done the first-footing at the old Spinner home. Honouring a tradition the first Spinners brought with them, Lennie had been the dark-haired stranger who had crossed the threshold carrying a lump of coal seconds after midnight on New Year's Eve, delivering good fortune for the following year. Shortly after Lennie entered, the guests considered their New Year's resolutions.

Svensen, who had felt the Santa Claus suit closing in on him at the kids' Christmas party, patted his middle and said he was embarking on a health-and-careful-eating kick and to look out for a slimmer Swede. "Starting tomorrow," he added, sitting down before a plate of Rachel Spinner's chunky, sugared shortbread and reducing it to a scattering of crumbs.

Miss Bell-Atkinson, patting her basset, Sarah, agreed to be more tolerant of Svensen and Conrad, his docile German shepherd. She was on her second dry sherry.

Shortly afterwards, she went out to get her purse from her car. Conrad was on three legs, the other one being cocked against the car's left rear wheel. Miss Bell-Atkinson rushed at the dog in his disadvantaged stance and kicked him sideways into a holly bush. She said that he was a beast and his owner was little better.

Inside, Rachel Spinner vowed to more easily bear fools, of which she firmly believes the Inlet has an inordinate number. She then watched, with witheringly diminishing patience, as Lennie, quite awash, did his annual impersonation of a one-man band, using only his mouth, nose and hands. His performance, especially the raspberried crescendo, is neither harmonious nor in very good taste. When he finished, and bowed, Rachel said, "You dolt."

Just prior to that, Rachel, with her Derwent Kennels in mind, had induced Scott McConville, the vet, to resolve that in future he would be less testy when called out in the small hours to attend a breached pup.

As Rachel finished berating Lennie, the phone rang. It was Froelich, howling that one of his Holstein calves was choking. Scott had disappeared. At the cries of a Froelich emergency he appeared from down the darkened hallway, muttering about "people and their bloody animals," and was followed shortly by Joanne Spinner, flushed of face.

Sebastian swore a sea-going oath that he would strive for less officiousness, a condition that frequently afflicts him when he dons the peaked cap to take tickets at the ferry booth. As he left in the early hours to prepare for the first docking of the *Gulf Queen*, cap squarely set, two of Wilson Spinner's ewes ambled past him.

Sebastian glanced about him, then, secure in the knowledge there were just the three of them: "Avast, you swabs!" he commanded. Then, "Snap it up, there!—Left! Left! Left, right, left! Rigggght turn!" And he marched off down the driveway, arms swinging, head and cap up.

The Brigadier said resolutions are rubbish. But he did concede to the young constable, who had dropped in for a noggin, that he perhaps should use a little more of his own side of the road while driving the Mini-minor.

The Brigadier prepared to leave and Nelson Spinner and Lennie Wilson stepped out to take the early morning air. Lennie earlier had submitted to the collective rush of resolve and tossed his last half-pack of smokes into the embers of the old year.

When Nelson stopped to light up a butt he had fished from his shirt pocket, Lennie, afloat in self-righteousness, kept walking, straight into the Brigadier's Mini which roared around the turnabout on the wrong side. Brakes squealed and Lennie jumped—but not quickly enough. A fender nudged him and he bounced into a convenient arbutus, dislocating his shoulder.

Now, a short time later, his right arm was cradled in a sling. Nelson passed the requested cigarette and supplied a light.

"No cracks," Lennie warned.

Nelson paused. Then he blew a smoke ring. "Happy New Year," he said.

Passport Predicament

Lennie Wilson showed Nelson Spinner the passport application form. "It's enough to make you cancel your trip," he said.

Lennie and Maggie were taking a holiday to mark 25 years of mercurial matrimony. Their last one was their honeymoon, in Seattle. This time their sights were on Spain, where Margarita Consuela Pereyra-Mendez Wilson still has family.

Lennie was pointing to the list of occupations the federal government accepts as guarantors.

"Minister of religion," Nelson read. Lennie considered the brief debate he'd had last week with the Reverend Randall Rawlings about church attendance. It had ended with Lennie explaining that he had never been a God-botherer and was not about to swell their numbers.

He went down the list.

Bank signing officer. Lennie shuddered. His last contact with the bank over in Richmond had concluded with Lennie advising the manager that given his quoted interest rates, he was the usurious spawn of a capitalistic monster that would soon meet its just end at the hands of the people, and that Lennie would take his business elsewhere.

"Engineer?" Nelson suggested. There was one, a fellow who worked for Hydro and had a place down past the Cedars. Lennie, on his way home from the Cedars' lounge one evening last summer, had stopped and offered extensive, loud, and persistent advice as the man adjusted his levels to plot the lines of a tricky curved and sloping driveway. Lennie wondered if the man would remember him, and decided, probably yes.

A school principal could sign it, Nelson pointed out. Lennie glanced up at his letter to the editor that *The Tidal Times* had published the previous week and which he had proudly taped to the basement wall. It was an unrelenting attack on the fat-cat, cream-fed administrators whose grossly-inflated salaries threaten to bring the school-tax payers to their knees.

It urged an immediate return to full-time classroom teaching by all principals and vice-principals, where they might once again dip their aristocratic and pampered snouts into a little chalk dust as a change from the public trough.

"I don't think so," Lennie said.

On principle, he would not approach a lawyer, also on Ottawa's list. Lennie's last brush with the legal profession was when he and Maggie had bought the house, years ago. The man had handled everything for them by mail from Victoria and billed them quite a chunk. Lennie grumbled, but paid up.

A month later the lawyer kept Lennie waiting 45 minutes beyond an appointment time for Lennie to ask him if there was anything he could legally do to the real estate agent who had neglected to mention the terminal condition of the roof, and who had recommended the lawyer. The lawyer said no, and Lennie said goodbye, and left. A week later he got a bill for $35. Two collection agencies have failed to pry it from him.

He dismissed judges, notaries public and police officers—the first because they once were lawyers, the second because they sounded like lawyers, the third simply because the young constable hadn't been on the island the two years that the guarantor is required to know the applicant.

"Which is probably just as well," Nelson noted.

There is currently no dentist in the Inlet, so that was out, and Dr. Timothy was on his annual vacation to the Turks and Caicos Islands.

Postmaster? Lennie pondered. Postmistress, it is. Thelma Spooner.

Lennie's oldest boy, Walter, has been spending a lot of time around Thelma's daughter, Heather. He did not want to seem to be encouraging that.

"That leaves a mayor," said Nelson. "And we don't have one."

"The Brigadier thinks he's the mayor," Lennie said. "Maybe we should let him sign it and then let Ottawa try telling him he's not."

The next day Nelson Spinner was in Vancouver.

"Thelma gave you an old form," he told Lennie when he got back. "The passport people have added two more occupations."

An hour later Lennie hoisted his broad-beamed bull terrier, Windy, into the pickup. He went over and patted the goat, then drove off toward Scott McConville's clinic.

"Vets," he said to himself. "That's more like it. And if Scott's not home, I can hit on Chief Jimmy Plummer."

The federal government had added animal doctors and Indian chiefs to the guarantors list.

"There may be intelligent life in Ottawa yet," Lennie said.

Rachel's Visitor

Rachel Spinner's nose wrinkled as a stream of cigarette smoke curled past her face. She was sitting up front on the *Gulf Queen*, in the non-smokers' section. Two teenage girls sitting behind her laughed.

Rachel turned around and measured them. They stared back and the one with the blonde hair—except for the path of magenta running back from her forehead—blew a smoke ring.

Rachel smiled at them and said, "There's a smokers' section further back, you know."

The reply from the blonde one was familiar, short, and crude. Rachel recalled, many years back, experimenting with the age-old rejoinder herself. The girl nudged her companion and snickered. The other one tossed her pitch-black hair and fashioned a smile that never quite reached her startlingly blue eyes.

A passing crew member told the blonde girl to douse her cigarette or leave. She sneered, then the two of them picked up small backpacks and bumped their way out.

The blonde one leaned over Rachel's seat. "Bye, granny," she said, and hooted.

The ferry docked at Spinner's Inlet and Rachel in the pickup trundled past the two girls as they strode jauntily up the wharf toward the road. The blonde one raised a single finger, the other turned a small, defiant face that held Rachel's eyes for a second.

Rachel turned into the Derwent Kennels. She muttered a couple of times about "a damned shame and a waste" as she organized the feeding schedule and cleaned up. She stayed a while with Greta Lass, her favourite setter bitch, and the four, month-old pups, and she put the two hard girls out of her mind.

She was on her way down to Logan's store in mid-afternoon when she passed the black-haired one. The girl was alone, sitting on her pack at the corner of Borrowdale Road.

She was still there when Rachel returned. She looked up as the truck approached, then quickly down again. Her bold mascara had smudged. Rachel slowed, then drove on. She stopped and reversed. Through the rolled-down window she said, "Where's your friend?"

The girl shrugged, and her shoulders, through her thin denim jacket, trembled.

"You've missed the ferry," Rachel said. "There's four hours to the next one. You'll freeze if you stay there. Better get in the truck," she added.

The girl looked up at her.

"Come on," Rachel said.

The girl turned away for a moment, then picked up her pack. She sat in silence as Rachel drove back to the kennels and she followed her into the house.

"Cup of tea," said Rachel, and the girl sat at the kitchen table.

"What's your name?"

"Penny," the girl said.

"Where is your friend?"

"She went with a couple of guys on motorbikes. I didn't want to go."

Rachel poured the tea. "I imagine your parents will be wondering about you," she said, pointing to the phone. "You'd better call them."

The girl shook her head. "It's not important."

She stood and walked to the living room and stopped before a collection of framed photographs on the mantel piece.

"Do you have a family?" she asked.

"Brothers and such," Rachel said. "I never married."

The girl moved closer to a faded snapshot of a stunningly beautiful young Rachel Spinner in a Second World War air-force-blue uniform of skirt, tunic and cap. Titian hair was tucked under the cap, and one hand rested against the sleek belly of a Spitfire. Rachel wore the two thin stripes of a second officer in the British Air Auxiliary, and a pilot's wings.

The girl studied the picture intently. Finally: "You were in the war?" she said. "Flying?"

Rachel chuckled. "A lot of women were. Ferry pilots. We flew up and down Britain, delivering all sorts of planes to airfields. How old are you?" she asked the girl.

"Sixteen."

"I was 20 then."

The girl moved on to the next picture. It was Rachel, this time in a sun-suit and her long hair flowing about her shoulders. Her head rested against the arm of a slim, dark-haired boy in RAF blues with flying officer's rings.

"I was going to marry him," Rachel said. "He went out one morning and never came back. I have his medals," she said, with a wry smile. Then, "Come on," she said. "I have to check the pups."

Rachel heard the girl's gasp of pleasure as she opened the door on Greta Lass and the velvety pups. Rachel held and patted the big gentle setter while the girl touched the pups, stroking them with her finger tips and making small, delighted sounds.

Finally Rachel leaned over. "It's time to go."

The girl was quiet during the drive to the ferry. She climbed down from the truck as the *Gulf Queen* nosed into the dock, and she turned to Rachel.

"Thank you," she said. "And . . . I'm sorry."

Rachel nodded. Then she said, "You know, Penny, there are times when those dogs are a bit much for one elderly lady. It would be nice occasionally to have an extra hand around the place."

The girl stared at her for a second, then a smile lit the small face. It was still there when she waved and trotted aboard as the last foot-passenger.

And That's the Law

The new Mountie captured everyone's attention within days of taking over. He had nodded but paid little attention when the departing constable advised him, "Feel your way. This place isn't in any of the books."

First he nailed the Brigadier, who had initially remarked favourably on the young fellow's academy-fresh pressed uniform and his positively glowing boots. When the lights and sirens erupted behind him the Brigadier dutifully swung the Mini-minor into the side and vigorously waved the patrol car on after its quarry.

The car stopped behind him and the constable got out. He was brusque in demanding the Brigadier's licence and registration, and crisp in his assessment of the Brigadier as a calamity waiting to occur. He said that while straddling the centre line may well keep one out of the ditches and away from lurking power poles, it also invites an early end, and he would have no more of it.

"The law is the law," he added.

The novelty of his *Québécois* accent in asking, " 'Ave we hunderstood?" failed to mute the Brigadier's feelings.

"The jumped-up young bugger!" he exploded, later, to Wilson and Barbara Spinner. "Bloody rookies!"

Miss Bell-Atkinson congratulated the Mountie, advising him that she was impressed with his attitude, that it was time certain people in the community were put straight and, with a pat on the back, to "keep up the good work, my boy." The next day he gave her a ticket for running the stop sign at the intersection of Ennerdale Road and Asby Lane. He lectured her briefly on her destructive potential while her identical, bespectacled, twin nephews, Henry and/or Harvey, perched on the rear seat like a set of petrified owls.

"He's not going to work out!" she announced minutes later, banging around in Logan's store. "You'd think the police would have something better to do, with all the crime in the world, wouldn't you?"

Charlie nodded, and slipped the five-dollar-a-square weekly football pools card under the refrigerated sausage bin. No one would ever describe Charlie as a bookie. It was just understood that a small commission went to providing the service, which sometimes stretched to accommodate the races at Exhibition Park and Cloverdale.

The Mountie was down at the ferry dock, listening politely and nodding occasionally as Harry the Phone gave him a run-down on the history of the Welsh in BC. The *Gulf Queen* docked and Harry went aboard to collect a package. The Mountie walked back up to the highway and put a $35 parking ticket on Harry's BC Tel van, which was parked under a "no parking at anytime" sign.

"Bloody rubbish, now that is," Harry sputtered, his Cambrian spirit astir, when he saw it. "I mean, you don't give parking tickets round 'ere, do you?"

He was reminded of the law.

The next night, the Mountie turned up at the Cedars pub five minutes after drink-up time. Jackson and Evelyn Spinner were on a rare night out and Evelyn was waiting for Jackson to finish up his cider. The Mountie went straight to Maurice behind the bar and advised him that there was a law concerning drinking hours and that he wasn't going to put up with it being breached. Jackson put down his half-full glass and he and Evelyn left. On the way out they wished the constable good night, and he nodded.

It got to the point where a nod was all anyone was exchanging with him. He just wouldn't get loose. Mind, if it hadn't been for his zealousness, he might still have been just nodding.

Young Edward Plummer blasted past him in his old Jeep, minus a muffler and burning up the road. The Mountie hit all his switches and took off after him. Edward turned quickly onto one of the trails that run down to the beach. At the end he hit the sand and kept going.

The Mountie hit it, too, and stopped, wheels churning, digging in the cruiser. He was just a car's length from the water and the tide was coming in. A couple of people drifted onto the beach lower down, and watched. Then a couple more.

The Mountie rocked the car, into first, into reverse, and back. Sand flew and the car sank further. Those watching saw him finger his walkie-talkie, then leave it. He tried rocking the car again. An advance wavelet rushed up and licked the front tire, and ran back.

The constable yanked off his hat, knuckled his hair, and put the hat back on. Another wave splashed the wheel. The Mountie looked all around. The watchers watched. He lifted his radio.

"Forget it," Edward Plummer said. He stepped off the path, the end of a winch cable in his hand. Jackson Spinner was behind him.

The spectators awarded a round of lively applause as the police cruiser was eased gently back onto the path and the sea water ran into and filled the depressions left by its wheels. Edward and Jackson left in the Jeep.

The next afternoon the constable, in jeans and sweater, strode into Logan's store and up to Charlie behind the counter. "I 'ear you are gamble on a football pool," he said, his face grim.

Charlie sighed. Then he shrugged, lifted the sausage bin and slid the card out. It was almost full. The constable studied it, then his hand came up with a folded ten-dollar bill.

"I'll 'ave that one and that one, please," he said.

Lottie's Luck

Joanne Spinner opened the door into the veterinary clinic, and halted. Scott McConville, a small pepper shaker in one hand, was poised over a quizzical, blue-grey Persian cat.

"Would you like the ketchup, too?" asked Joanne.

The cat, its feathery tail suddenly a lash, stalked off.

Scott blushed. "I, ah, was trying to make it sneeze. If a cat sneezes in the house on the day before the wedding. . . . "

"It's Aunt Lottie!" Joanne cut him off. "She's got to you! Or maybe it's in your veins. Maybe I'm marrying into a coven, for God's sake!"

No one had expected Scott's great-aunt Lottie from Charlottetown to actually attend the young couple's wedding, which was to be a relatively quiet affair at the little Church in the Vale. But she phoned, and two days later they met her at the Vancouver airport.

That's where it started. On the way to the car the little woman nimbly and diligently stepped over every crack in the cement sidewalk. In the car she turned sharply to Joanne and said "You'll be wearing nothing green for the wedding, I dare say? Unlucky to marry with green. Unless you're one of those Irish, which you're not."

It was more instruction than question. Joanne mentally stripped her bride-figure of the jade earrings she had been considering wearing.

Lottie was staying with Joanne's family. On the second evening she darted into Joanne's room as the bride-to-be was slipping the wedding dress over her head.

"Get it off!" Lottie screamed, and Joanne leaped out of the folds of silk. "You don't try on the dress before the day," Lottie snapped. "Bad luck."

Joanne said, "And what if I find it's not right on the day?"

"I'll fix it," Lottie said. "A stitch in the dress before the wedding brings luck, anyway. Anybody knows that."

The three words became a daily routine in the week leading up to the wedding: "Anybody knows that."

Joanne's mother, Melinda, watched bemused one night as Lottie emptied her purse onto the kitchen table, spread out a heap of coins and started turning them over, one by one.

"Turn your money on the new moon, don't you?" Lottie said, opening the door to point to the lunar crescent in the inky night sky. "Anybody knows that."

She surprised Joanne's father, Dixon, by advising him that his habitual early-morning humming of the "Londonderry Air" was an invitation to disaster.

"Sing before breakfast, cry before night," she warned.

She also caught his attention when she remarked on his well

thinned hair and how actually simple restoration is. But his interest waned when Lottie explained that the effective cure for baldness, verified over centuries, is an unstinting application of goose droppings.

Lottie hovered over every laying of the table after once catching two knives lying crossed at lunch time. She insisted on being the last to bed every night, so that she'd be sure the dead embers would be cleaned out from the big stone fireplace.

"No need to invite trouble," she explained.

Anyone who had a boiled egg for breakfast soon learned they'd better not leave the table without first punching a hole through the empty shell with a spoon.

"Anybody knows that," Lottie said.

As the wedding day approached she bombarded Joanne with a storm of warnings and advice. "Don't let a dog pass between the two of you on the day. That can be fatal. Have a good cry on the morning. It's lucky. And make sure you're out of the church door before him after the ceremony—first out runs the house."

"She's bizarre," Joanne told Scott in the middle of the week. "She knows every superstition ever recorded, and some of her own, and she lives by all of them."

Scott shook his head. "Actually she's mellowed quite a bit. When I was three and still wetting the bed she was going to feed me three roast mice. My mother stopped her. I remember when I had the whoopin' cough. She put a hairy caterpillar in a little bag and hung it round my neck. I still get the willies when I see one." He had assured Joanne there was nothing hereditary in Lottie's obsession.

Now he looked sheepishly at the pepper shaker, and set it down.

"Well, I mean, it can't do any harm, can it?"

Joanne shook her head, a clearing action. She walked up and kissed him. "See you at the church," she said, and left.

Halfway down the driveway a small black kitten shot out across in front of her. Joanne crossed her fingers.

As she drove on, thinking of last-minute details, she found herself murmuring, "Something old, something new, something borrowed. . . " She stopped. Then finished the rhyme, ". . . something blue," and chuckled.

"Well, everybody knows that," she said.

A Witching Well

For years Froelich has grazed his few Holsteins on the five acres adjoining his property. The land until just recently belonged to a Burnaby doctor who never used it. One reason for that was the general belief that there was no water to be had.

The belief has been well fostered by Froelich, whose mouth tightened when he saw the young musician with his slip of a wife, and their two kids bouncing about like ping-pong balls. They were looking over the property with Evelyn Spinner, recently licensed to sell real estate.

Evelyn introduced them at the fence. "Jason and Peggy Slater, and Sandra and Ben."

"You're not thinking of buying that, are you?" Froelich said, with a wave of the hand.

Slater smiled and said indeed he was and had picked a spot for the house.

"It's dry," Froelich said. "It's as bad as all the others outside of mine."

Slater said that's what he'd like to discuss. Froelich has the best water in the Inlet, his well standing full at any time of the year and with no apparent limit to it. He drains and fills his swimming pool at will and the stuff just keeps coming. Others nearby have a modest and sometimes seasonal supply.

"I was thinking that I could perhaps buy water from you," Slater said. "Run a line with a meter from your well and I'd pay whatever. . . . "

"Not a chance," Froelich said, and a thin, small smile drifted over his mouth.

"We wouldn't need all that much. . . . "

"No," said Froelich, and he walked away.

"Told you," Evelyn shrugged. "Miserable bugger," she added.

"Has it ever been drilled?" Slater asked.

Evelyn shook her head. "You don't do that casually. Expensive. Actually, I don't know if it's been witched, even."

"Witched?" the musician replied. "Witched?"

Froelich's cows were grazing when the Slaters returned the next weekend. Evelyn was with them and so was big Iorwerth Davies, who maintains he has lines going back to Owain Glyn Dwr. He's been witching water for over 60 years and they say that during the North African campaign his outfit was the only one that washed and shaved on a daily basis.

Iorwerth cut a slim, Y-shaped limb from a young maple. He held the arms of the Y, one in each hand, and extended the long piece horizontally in front of him. The Slaters watched, intrigued, and skeptical.

Iorwerth paced along the sides of the property, down the middle, and criss-crossed. The maple rode steadily at chest height. He covered two-thirds of the property.

"Not a trace," he said.

"If there's water, I'll find it," he had told the Slaters. The witching fee of $50 would be paid only when drilling confirmed his find.

He was at the bottom of a short, gorse-covered slope when he stopped and called. "Here. Jason, come and feel it."

The musician hurried over. Iorwerth gripped the maple branch, which quivered in his big-knuckled hands. The tip pointed down.

Slater reached out and grasped one side of the forked limb, and gasped. It was pulling his hand and arm down. He checked Iorwerth's right hand. It was rock steady.

"There's your water," Iorwerth said. Later the musician asked Froelich to move his cattle as a drilling rig would be in the next weekend.

"Or I could still offer to buy. . . . "

"Forget it!" Froelich snapped and stalked off.

He ignored the young man's friendly wave a week later and watched as the rig was set up just after noon.

"Forty feet," the operator called an hour later. At $8.50 a foot. Froelich watched, and sneered.

"Eighty feet," the man said in the late afternoon. Not a drop. He packed up for the day and resumed the next morning. Froelich watched.

"A hundred and one," the driller announced, and Slater winced. Froelich laughed.

"A hundred and—there she goes!"

The water was clear, clean, and sweet.

"Sixty gallons a minute," the driller said later. "That's one of the best since Froelich's." He tossed a can of beer to the laughing young musician and, "What d'y' say there, Froelich!" he called across the pasture.

Froelich had been gripping the fence rail. Now he stomped off into the house. In the kitchen he rattled around and poured a biggish rye over ice and went to mix it. He turned the tap and there was a gurgle and a burp, then a spurt, and finally a listless sort of trickle that apparently was not going to get any bigger.

Home, Sweet Home

The return of Samson Spinner was greeted with unbridled delight by the Spinner family. Miss Bell-Atkinson was not so impressed.

"We get *him* back, and in the same week Dr. Timothy says he's leaving us. Rather a shabby trade, I would say."

Samson, named for his great great-grandfather and founder of the Canadian branch of the Spinner family, had been away four years this time, and might be ready to settle down.

Miss Bell-Atkinson was at the ferry dock when Samson strode off to be greeted by his parents, Wilson and Barbara, and the rest of the Spinners. Samson fastened his eyes on Miss Bell-Atkinson, threw out his arms as if to embrace her, and advanced. She gasped, and side-stepped, and Samson stopped and hooted.

"Buffoon, like the rest of them," she said, and resumed her fretting about Dr. Timothy.

The doctor and his wife Morag moved to the Inlet three years ago and they fit right in. Morag became a pillar of the Inlet Players, an organization that is one of Miss Bell-Atkinson's main reasons for drawing breath. A couple of weeks ago Dr. Timothy called Evelyn Spinner and abruptly requested that she put the house up on the market. He gave her an asking price and added bleakly, "or whatever you can get."

What it came down to, as Nelson Spinner learned, was that the doctor and Morag had had an incendiary confrontation about when and whether to take off for the weekend in Vancouver and finally Morag, her Celtic blood bubbling, said there'd be no more arguments like that because she was damn-well moving back to the mainland and he could damn-well go with her or damn-well stay here until he damn-well grew moss.

"It's a standoff," said Nelson. "Appparently, intelligence and social standing are no impediment to pigheadedness. If the house sells before they cool off, they'll be gone. Probably regretting it, but gone."

"I have a couple coming to see it tomorrow," Evelyn said.

Samson was strolling past the doctor's house when Evelyn and the couple arrived, and he tagged along.

"Fine-looking place," the man said.

"Oh, it was, indeed it was," Samson said.

The man stopped. "Was? What do you mean 'was'?"

"Eh? Oh, nothing, nothing," replied Samson. He gazed toward the rear of the house. "I'm sure there's no trace now anyway," he said. "Of course to a doctor anyway . . . " He stopped and shrugged the subject away.

"Trace of what?" the man said very quietly.

Samson examined some drifting clouds. "Well, actually, ah, blood," he said. "And stuff."

"Stuff?" the man whispered.

"The other owners," Samson allowed. "Terrible row one night. Drinking you know. Big man. Shovel, they say . . . awful." He shuddered.

"Harriet!" the man called. "Harriet!"

Evelyn phoned Dr. Timothy later. "The woman seemed very interested but her husband wouldn't even step inside. I've another couple coming on the weekend," she said.

Samson was passing and stopped to chat with the woman as Evelyn discussed the bay windows with the man.

"Good school, oh, yes," Samson said to the question.

"And the neighbours?"

Samson frowned slightly, then cleared his brow. "Oh, I think he's fine now," he said. "Yes," nodding, "I'm sure he is."

"Who?" she said quickly. "What?" And, "What do you mean, 'now'?"

"Old whatsisname." Samson gestured vaguely over toward a stand of fir. "Never *touched* anybody, mind. All—well—show and tell, you know . . . the old raincoat and nothing under it. An open and shut case, you might say," he chuckled.

The woman blinked. "Thank you," she said, and marched off to-

61

ward her husband. Evelyn gave Samson a mildly quizzical look as the couple left.

"This time the husband liked it," she told Dr. Timothy on the phone later. "But the woman. . . . "

"Evelyn," he cut in. "Listen, we, uh, we've changed our minds. We're taking the house off the market."

Miss Bell-Atkinson left Logan's store and frowned as Samson Spinner coasted by in an aging van. He blew her a kiss and she wrinkled her face in distaste. Then she smiled happily as Dr. Timothy's car appeared and he slowed and waved. "Thank heavens," she breathed, "that there are still *some* people you know will do the right thing."

Partners

Svensen chuckled and waved to his old partner at the head of the car-deck crowd as the *Gulf Queen* nosed in to the dock. Jensen lifted a hand in return and his face, a biography of rough roads, formed a crooked grin. The two clasped hands just as Froelich passed them, going aboard.

"So, Jensen, gonna dry out again, are we?" Froelich called for the benefit of anyone within earshot.

The look on the older man's face escaped Froelich, a stranger to the subtleties of life. It did not escape Svensen, nor the half-dozen others nearby.

In their prime together, the two Swedes had cut broad swaths through a goodly part of BC's rainforest, and an immoderate number of the province's beer stops. Now Jensen has a room on Powell Street, maintaining he's seen enough woods to last him. But when the loneliness of the crowded city and the spurious friendship of the bottle start closing in, he rises up and announces to Svensen he is coming over. It is understood he will be attempting to stay on the wagon.

Svensen muttered an unkindness at Froelich's retreating back, and pointed Jensen to the pickup. He pulled into Nelson Spinner's place to return a nail gun. As they stopped, Samson Spinner came backwards out through the screen door, with an opened beer bottle in each hand, saw the Swedes, turned and re-entered the house and came out, hands empty. Jensen grunted as they drove away.

A couple of days later, the pair sauntered around the craft fair at the community hall. The Reverend Randall Rawlings' wife nodded as they approached her stall, and draped a large dish towel across the half-dozen bottles of blackberry, apple, and plum wines on display. She smiled guilelessly at Jensen. A rather long breath escaped Jensen's lips, but he said nothing.

They went to the bingo on the Friday and eased casually into the card room afterward, where a poker game was coming to life. After the first two hands Nelson Spinner excused himself and was back in a few minutes. Shortly after that the Brigadier was out for five minutes and returned dabbing his mouth. Others went out and returned, Lennie Wilson preceded by a rattling burp.

The Swedes left. "They think I'm a bloody deficient of some sort!" Jensen snapped.

A couple of days later, they sat among the crowd ready for the Pioneer's Firewood Chop-off. Five piles of alder logs that would make a cord each when bucked and split, stood in the field behind the school. The firewood goes to Pioneer Hall, the small senior citizens' complex. Teams of two stood at four of the piles, each pair equipped with a chainsaw, axes and mauls. The brothers-in-law Jackson Spinner and Edward Plummer were down for the fifth but hadn't shown.

"Gotta get it going," Samson Spinner called, checking both his watch and the line of threatening clouds. "We'll go with four."

Jensen rose to his feet. "Five," he said. "Come on," he said, nudging the Swede. He strode to the pickup and lifted out Svensen's saw. There was one maul there, and he borrowed another, hefting it for feel. People laughed and several applauded as the two old loggers took their places.

"Start your saws!" Samson shouted, and the five motors coughed and jumped into snarling life. Jensen fed gas and grinned at Svensen. The Brigadier raised his .303 and as the shot crashed out the saws bit down, and thick streams of oblong woodflakes poured out and fell, forming little pointed hills.

A pickup skidded up and Jackson Spinner and Edward Plummer tumbled out, but Samson waved them away, and pointed to the Swedes.

Jensen felt his frame moving to the rhythm of a half-century of working in the woods as he planted his feet and flexed his knees. The chiselled teeth flicked away the grey-green bark and then sank in and amputated length after eye-measured length. As fast as they fell, Svensen was at them, using one fat butt end as a splitting block. Jensen finished bucking at the same time as young James Plummer who was working with his twin, John.

Then Jensen picked up the other maul. The wedge-blade rose and fell and flashed, and chunks of cream-white alder flew and dropped on a pile that grew at a rate that few there had ever seen.

For a while the crowd deferred, through silence, to an artist, but soon they started applauding, rhythmically with Jensen's flow, and when he finished they gave him a standing, crashing ovation. His face was scarlet and glossy with running sweat as he looked around at the others, who stopped their belated chopping to join in the applause.

The modest prize was always the same, and it was sitting on a nearby cedar stump. A case of beer. Jensen examined it for a moment, then stepped over to the stump. He popped the box open, snapped the cap off a bottle with the edge of the maul, and drained the contents. Then he wiped his mouth on his sleeve and turned to Svensen.

"Just the one," he said, "for the old days," and the two old loggers slapped hands and laughed out loud.

A Dog and Its Boy

Sebastian Whittle turned away and started fiddling around in the ticket booth when he saw young Timmy Brannigan trudging down the ferry wharf with the dog. The dog was going, and damned good riddance to it.

It had been bad enough when the Brannigans moved in and rented the old house next door. Seven of them and their harassed mother from somewhere up the coast, and no sign of a father. About as much discipline as Saturday-night soldiers. But the dog had capped it. A great gormless creature with a permanently ingratiating grin, and looking like a cross between a muskox and a haystack. It had attached itself to the youngest Brannigan, Timmy, who had christened it O'Toole.

For openers, it had taken Sebastian's best ferry uniform cap off the seat of his truck and reduced it to mush. Sebastian had warned the Brannigans about further transgressions. The very next morning, the dog made a forced entry to the Whittles' kitchen and knocked off six lamb chops that Marion Whittle had just placed in a marinade of rosemary and lime juice.

"I'll shoot the stupid bugger if it comes over here again," Sebastian had advised his neighbours, and he repeated his intent to Constable Jean LaFleur.

And then, the other day, the pullet went. A mound of feathers and fluff that had recently contained one of Sebastian's prized Rhode Island Reds was all that remained.

"He just wanted to play with it," Timmy Brannigan had pleaded.

"Play? He ate the bloody thing!" Sebastian exploded, and he went for the gun. Jean LaFleur had interceded with the compromise. "They will find a good 'ome for him from the Richmond pound," he told Timmy. "We'll put him on the ferry." And he had tousled the kid's hair.

The boy hesitated now as he drew abreast of the ticket booth and he turned his head, the blue bold eyes large in the too-thin face. Sebastian frowned down at his cashbox, and the boy and the dog moved on.

The boy went and sat on the edge of the dock, his arm around the great beast's neck. He turned up the collar of his frayed denim jacket against the bite of the sudden southeaster. The two of them gazed out across the water, and somewhere around the point the *Gulf Queen* blasted notice of her approach.

"Bloody menace it was," Sebastian muttered. He looked up and watched as the boy tightened his grip on the dog and hugged its great maned head closer to his own small face. Sebastian lost count of the money in the cashbox, swore, and banged the lid shut. He started counting tickets.

A bicycle skidded to a stop and Willie, Sebastian's youngest, stepped off. It was a new bicycle, all shiny paint and chrome. Willie wore his thick quilted jacket, jeans, and high-cut Nike runners. He nodded to his dad, then waved across the dock. "Hey, Timmy."

The Brannigan youngster turned and smiled and nodded. His eyes took in Willie and lingered on the bike. He glanced at Sebastian, then turned away. His arm was locked around the big dog's neck.

The *Gulf Queen* nudged in to the dock and a crew member yelled at Sebastian to get the lead out and the ramp down. Sebastian stepped out of the ticket booth and danced sideways as the squad car whispered to a stop and Constable Jean LaFleur stepped out.

The young policeman gave a curt nod, then walked over and stopped by the Brannigan youngster. He made a joke that Sebastian couldn't hear, and the boy forced a smile while he brushed away hair that seemed to keep falling across his eyes.

Young Willie had crossed the dock, unwrapping a chocolate bar as he went. He broke it and gave half to the other boy. Then Willie broke a square off his own and offered it to the dog. The great fan of a tail thumped on the dock, and a length of pink tongue slobbered on Willie's hand. The Brannigan kid laughed, then broke his chocolate into pieces and fed them to the dog. He kept on brushing his hair out of his eyes.

The first officer yelled from the car deck for Sebastian to get his butt moving. Sebastian yelled something back that got lost in the wind, then he marched across the dock. Constable Jean LaFleur looked at Sebastian and looked away. Willie looked at Sebastian, then at the Brannigan kid, then out into the Inlet. The Brannigan youngster looked up and held Sebastian's gaze. Then his eyes slipped away again. The dog snuffled at Sebastian's hand and wriggled its behind.

"The thing is a damned menace," Sebastian said.

The first officer invited Sebastian to lower the ramp.

"A chicken killer, in fact," Sebastian added.

Willie Whittle looked sideways at Timmy Brannigan, then up into the bruised sky. Sebastian took a deep breath and exhaled. Then he pointed a finger at the dog and he spoke, slowly, the words separated by stern pauses.

"No... more... chickens."

The Brannigan kid blinked. Then his eyes widened. Constable Jean LaFleur sputtered. Willie Whittle punched the Brannigan kid on the shoulder and whooped.

"No more chickens," the kid said, and galloped back up the wharf, and they heard him yell into its great woolly face as he ran, "No more bloody chickens!"

Miss Weaver

Samson Spinner was locked into a stream of traffic wheeling down Granville Street toward the city when he first saw the old lady. She was about five blocks ahead, dressed in something long and white, in the middle of the intersection.

Several cars swung to avoid her as she wavered, first stepping this way, then that. All went past her. A car about six ahead of Samson finally stopped, halting the flow. A tall man got out, took the old woman's arm and guided her to the sidewalk.

Samson sighed, relieved, and checked his watch. He had 35 minutes to drop off the dog-show entries for Rachel, his aunt. She was entering two of the setters and refused to trust the papers to the mail. Samson had assured her he'd have them to the downtown office before the afternoon deadline.

"Guaranteed," he'd said.

The tall man patted the old lady on the arm, climbed into his car, and drove off. The traffic moved again. The lady, in what Samson saw was a ragged terry-cloth dressing gown, teetered out into the road again.

Samson banged the car to a stop and jumped out. A big Detroit product swerved out from behind him, horn blaring, and a storm of insults blasted from its open windows as it screamed away. Others swung round him, in both lanes, many of the drivers mouthing. Samson eased the lady over to the corner.

"Stay there," he said. "I'm coming right back."

She looked up at him and smiled through large, stained teeth. Her hair was yellowing white and it barely covered a scalp that was scaling, almost crusted. She carried a musty odour.

Samson slewed the car off Granville onto Matthews, and parked. He got to her just as she was adventuring off the sidewalk again.

"Now," he said, and his fingers touched her dry twig of a wrist. "Where are you going?"

She smiled at him again, a distance in her eyes, and looked down at a pair of very old, pointed black shoes. A rolled-down nylon stocking flopped over one, like a small, dead animal.

"The . . . the money place," she said. "Same as the last time I got out. . . . "

Traffic streamed past, some drivers slowing down at the sight of the odd pair to look and laugh.

"What's your name?" Samson asked, checking his watch. Thirty minutes. Plenty of time.

"Miss Weaver," she said, and added quickly, "My father came from Ireland and he settled in Chilliwack. He had two thousand dollars . . . or acres. He was a fine man. I was a, ah. . . . " She sought for the word in the air. " . . . children . . . school." Her voice faded and she stared into her own world. Then, "They're always watching you," she said, fluttering a mottled hand vaguely off into Shaughnessy.

Samson knew some of the older houses were given over to nursing homes. He had no idea which. Nor did she. "Somewhere," she said.

He checked her purse. There was a bankbook for Charlotte

Weaver at a downtown branch. He visualized her crossing Granville Bridge.

"My hip hurts," she said.

He looked up and down Granville for a police car. Nothing. He walked her gently over to the car and sat her down in the passenger seat, leaving the door open.

" Are we going to the . . . money place?" she asked. Then, drifting again, "They make nice cookies but they never let you get out."

A young woman got off a bus and came toward them. She started back when Samson approached and asked her if she lived nearby. He pointed across to the old face, and explained.

She nodded. "I'll call the police. They usually can get them back home." Samson checked his watch. Twenty minutes.

She tried to rise up from the car, but couldn't. Samson talked to her and she sat back. She gazed up at him, and a line of spittle tracked down her chin. She grinned, the wrinkles folding into each other and making way for the stained teeth.

"I'm not afraid of you," she said. "They keep me in my room, you know."

He checked his watch and his stomach muscles clenched. The woman from the bus came back. "They said they'll get here right away. You can wait, can't you?" She was already moving away.

"You're a nice man," the old voice said. "Are you his son?"

Samson nodded. "Sure."

"You look like him," she said.

A patrol car slid around the corner and two young officers stepped out. They took his name and address and thanked him for staying with her.

"Sorry we took so long," the driver said. "We'll get her home now."

It was some time later that Samson phoned Rachel. He got only as far as saying he'd missed the entry deadline, and her voice came down the line like sharpened steel:

"The very best I can say, Samson, is that you are damned inconsiderate!" she snapped. And he winced as she cracked down the telephone.

Prices and Values

The charity auction drew a spirited crowd to the old Spinner yard and back porch. Nelson Spinner paced about before it opened, practising the auctioneer's patter as he perceives it:

"Hey! Who'll gimmee five, gimmee five, got six, gimmee seven, gimmee eight, gimmee more, much more, gimmee more. . . . "

Svensen was one of the first there with his donation, a very old carpenter's belt bristling with an amazing array of hand tools, some of which still work.

He stayed on one spot, eyes on the belt and spooky as a squirrel, until the bidding opened, at which point he slipped into his Depression state of mind—the one common to those who survived the breadlines of the 30s. It says you don't throw anything out, because it might come in useful sometime. The Swede actually straightens and saves bent nails. He flew up a huge and panicking hand and bellowed, "Twenty-five dollars!"—two and a half times his own reserve price— and retained ownership handily.

Miss Bell-Atkinson had provided a set of faintly yellowing linen bedsheets bearing a typed card that claimed the sheets had once slept next to "Royal persons."

"Prob'ly King Kong," said Lennie Wilson.

A puzzled Mrs. Brigadier was eventually handed the sheets and relieved of $15 after repeatedly waving to Nelson, whom she hadn't seen for ages and who she thought looked just splendid up there talking ever so quickly to the crowd.

Thelma Spooner, the postmistress, bid successfully on an old steamer trunk donated by the Reverend Randall Rawlings. Thelma endlessly reads paperback romances. In the last one, a sea captain had relentlessly retained a lost lover's negligee "in a sturdy, leather-bound chest" while he roamed life's oceans in search of her. The trunk was fastened with binder twine. Thelma cut through it, lifted the lid and peeped in. There were 19 mildewing paperback romances, including the one about the captain.

Lennie Wilson tried to unload Silas, the goat, which hasn't been right since Lennie poured the metric-measured weed-killer wrong and then put Silas out to graze. The animal walks either in circles or sideways. Lennie shouted that one of Miss Bell-Atkinson's twin nephews, Henry or Harvey, had bid on Silas and he attempted to have the creature imposed on them for $11.

Henry, or Harvey, demonstrated lavishly how he had simply been picking his nose; the other scuttled away and hid behind his aunt, who told Lennie to shut up. Nelson finally ruled that the goat was damaged and therefore ineligible.

A brisk bout of bidding ended with Elliott Smalley paying $65 for an oil portrait of a Haida princess, and leaving quickly with it. Barbara Spinner, who'd placed the painting out on the porch briefly while she washed down a wall, chased Elliott in the pickup down to the Cedars pub. Before she brought the painting home, the frame was badly cracked and Elliott was hurt on the shins.

"Watch it," Barbara said to Nelson when she got back.

Jean LaFleur, the young Mountie who is slowly overcoming his shyness, watched anxiously as his item came up. It was a delicately carved and painted wooden doll in the colourful costume of a 1700s Quebec peasant girl, everything handmade by Jean. The bidding started slowly and the constable blushed as Froelich's grating voice declared ". . . always peasants, anyway."

That's when Jackson Spinner and his brothers-in-law, Chief Jimmy Plummer's sons, stepped in and bounced bids off each other until the doll went for $55. Edward Plummer gave Jean the thumbs-up sign and the Mountie grinned.

Jackson offered Froelich a very different signal.

Evelyn Spinner directed Jackson as he bid on a neglected but superbly made old pine cradle. When the young pair collected it, Nelson said, "And about time," and winked as Evelyn blushed.

Nelson left until last two fluffy Persian kittens, sitting in a state of perpetual surprise in a wire cage. The donor was Scott McConville, the vet. He had included a smart wicker carrying basket and a year's free doctoring. The basket alone looked to be worth $20.

Any number of people had seen the Martin girls, Jillian and Julie, transfixed before the kittens, digging into their Strawberry Shortcake purses, blonde heads close together.

Their own kitten, Samantha, had met an ugly and untimely end two weeks ago under the back wheels of a visiting camper, and *The Tidal Times* had since run three letters to the editor about banning tourists.

The bidding opened at $1.50 and ended abruptly after young Julie bounced to her feet and piped, "Two dollars and ninety five cents— that's nearly three dollars!"

"Sold to the young lady for $2.95," Nelson ruled instantly.

Scott, incredulous, turned to his wife, until recently Joanne Spinner. "Two dollars and ninety five—!"

She laughed and gave him a shove. "Shut up," she said. "Sometimes, charity stays at home."

State of the Arts

Elliott Smalley, owner, editor, and everything else at *The Tidal Times*, pondered a lead sentence for his report on the outdoor summer concert organized by Miss Bell-Atkinson. The word "uneven" kept popping up. Miss Bell-Atkinson had promoted the event as "an opportunity to express our cultural awareness" and had invited participants.

She set the tone she expected by putting up first Henry and Harvey, her twin nephews, with a pair of matching violins. They managed a technically adequate and emotionally impoverished version of Paganini's "Duetto Amoroso" while she conducted. The audience was deprived of the closing bars when Nelson Spinner sat on the Swede's accordion down in the second row of seats.

"Ah, a critique," said Miss Bell-Atkinson, with a smile that would have etched glass.

The next item was billed as "An Alpine Adventure." It was Froelich, in lederhosen, a horn from some long-departed creature stuck under his arm, yodelling like a cut bullock while his haunted-looking wife clattered away at the piano in a tuneless and fruitless effort to keep time with him.

"Quite nice," Miss Bell-Atkinson judged coolly.

"My arse," countered Nelson, and added, "and that's a critique."

Young Charlie Wilson and Jason Slater put the thing back on an even keel for a while. Jason is with the symphony and Charlie has been playing with the youth orchestra in town since they heard him on his flute in the spring.

Jason brought out a sax and Charlie a clarinet and they enchanted the audience for 20 minutes while ranging from Brahms to boogie, in what Elliott chose happily to call a musical rainbow. After that the clouds, you could say, drifted in.

The young Martin girls were up for a guitar duet but entered into a conflict over who would sit where on the stage. The oldest, Jillian, plumped herself down and got off three chords of "Red River Valley" before little Julie, who is known least of all for her forbearance, knocked her off the chair and part-way out of her red buckle shoes. Jillian yelled, one guitar splintered, and the performance ended with Julie pronouncing near the open mike a decidedly gritty two-syllable description of her weeping sibling.

Miss Bell-Atkinson felt control slipping away, like a disappearing dream. She latched onto a flicker of hope when Thelma Spooner, postmistress and church organist, sat up to the piano and the Reverend Randall Rawlings stepped up beside her. They were billed as Hymn and Her, which might have alerted Miss Bell-Atkinson.

Thelma played a Sunday-sounding chord and Miss Bell-Atkinson's face flirted with a smile. The smile froze as Thelma half-turned to the audience and broke, simultaneously, into a simpleton's grin and a hideously adulterated version of the "Black Bottom", while Rawlings leaped about like a stork in heat.

"Wasn't that interesting," said Miss Bell-Atkinson through tightening lips as people replaced themselves on their chairs.

She turned then and watched with glazed fascination as Lennie Wilson hove into view straddling a horse borrowed from Chief Jimmy Plummer, plinking a ukelele and singing, very badly, "Don't Fence Me In."

She had, quite reasonably, rejected Lennie's one-man-band act— which he does on New Year's Eve, using only his hands, mouth, and nose—as being unusually offensive.

Lennie slurred words and was loose in the saddle as the old black stud creaked to a stop dead centre before the platform, got really comfortable and allowed itself a prolonged and copious relief.

Miss Bell-Atkinson missed the rest of the show: Wilson Spinner's recitation of "Young Lochinvar", the Swede howling a thoroughly off-key "Danny Boy", and Nelson playing the spoons on his head. She said she felt the need to lie down.

Elliott frowned down at the typewriter and started pecking tentatively.

"Culture," he wrote, "must surely be a state of mind. . . . "

Peace Walks

The Parade for Peace got off to a shaky start because of the bumper stickers, and it proceeded steadily downhill. The parade was instigated by Singlestar, a fading flower child whose conversation still consists mainly of "Like, man, y'know?"

He makes the stickers himself and retails them for $1.95, pocketing about $1.50 on each. A couple of badly smudged ones he stuck surreptitiously on the cars of his natural antagonists, such as the Brigadier. "Honk If You Love Peace," they read.

The five cars started honking well before the parade staggered into motion in front of Logan's store. They continued joyously on down the road and got louder as the line slowed down at Pioneer Hall, the small seniors' complex.

Four of the old people came out and shouted "Shut up!" and "Bugger off!" They then became very rude and issued some quite graphic instructions to Singlestar when he tried to sell them peace buttons for a dollar.

The parade drivers honked their appreciation as the confrontation escalated. Other seniors came out, advanced on Singlestar and began throwing items at him—grapefruit skins and other softening stuff— until reluctantly he signalled the retreat.

"Peace!" he shouted as he ducked and left, and "Bollocks!" came the answer. The parade moved on, but all was not well.

Miss Bell-Atkinson, whose mandate it is to miss nothing, was in the middle of the handful of marchers, keeping a stern eye on things. Twice she commanded a runny-nosed child to stop treading on her heels, and when it persisted, fetched it a sharp, backhand blow.

Immediately a hairy young man called her an antediluvian hag and assured her she would be right up front of those going to the wall when the people became the power. He then flashed an ingratiating two-finger sign and chimed "Peace, brothers" at Nelson Spinner and Lennie Wilson who sat on a fence rail reviewing the parade.

Nelson and Lennie responded with the reversed version of the Churchillian V-sign made popular by British soldiers in the Second World War. It signifies a vulgar opposition to things in general, and definitely includes anything resembling an organized march.

The line stuttered along, and the father of young Julie and Jillian Martin was admonished by a Singlestar disciple, dressed in an army surplus combat jacket, for his manner of firmly keeping the girls in order.

"They are not your children, you know," the young man advised Paul Martin. "They are just on loan to you," and he turned cryptic eyes in a vaguely skyward direction. Paul eyed the thrift-shop combat jacket. As a younger man, he had ventured to England to test his mettle and finished up doing three years in the Parachute Regiment's Third Battalion.

He asked the Singlestar clone if he thought The Loan had also included the diaper-changing and the three-AM-to-five-AM burp patrols, and he gently pushed the man away and told him to tend his business. The fellow had been knitting as he marched along and he started waving the needles around and shouting. He was still waving one, though with diminished vigour, when he landed up against a cedar stump with an unhealthy sounding thud.

"And peace on you, friend," Paul said. He left the march and took the girls for an ice cream.

Others were leaving the march, especially as they saw Singlestar advancing up the line with a collection bucket and his gap-toothed smile. The cars had all gone absent at the Cedars pub.

The parade wavered to a halt outside the Legion, where Singlestar had planned on delivering his speech on The Threat Behind The Uniform. The audience, however, was thin. There remained two of his disciples, three curious tourist kids and Svensen's German shepherd, Conrad. Singlestar counted them up, shrugged and checked the collection bucket.

"Listen," he said, a little later to the Legion steward. "Like, man, do you guys serve, ah, non-members?"

Sporting Spirit

As usual, the two events that drew the most interest at the Spinner's Inlet Sports Day were the gurning contest and the fell race. Both events are traditions of Cumberland, the northern English county that sent the first Spinners westward in the 1850s.

The fells are the Lakeland hills, where the race is from a meadow in the valley, up to a marker and back down. Here, the race is up Spinner's Mountain, the 500-foot-high hill overlooking the Inlet.

Gurning is where you stick your head through a horse collar and pull the ugliest possible face. Lennie Wilson insisted that Miss Bell-Atkinson, who did not compete, but did walk past, was the hands-down winner by virtue of his claim that her face would stop a row of clocks. Others said the honour should go to the Swede who, as announcer, jokingly put his head through the collar and gave his very best smile.

The fell race is always placed in Nelson Spinner's charge, and he maintains that people take it far too lightly. He advised his nephew

Jackson that he'd be expected to enter, and he told the three Plummer boys it was their duty to run, to maintain the tradition of such legendary Indian distance runners as Tom Longboat. He ignored their argument that Longboat was an Iroquois from back east and that on the west coast, young native men are more inclined to canoeing.

"Tom would have expected it of you," he said, and put their names down.

He collared young Charlie Wilson, Sebastian from the ferry booth, Scott McConville and the Reverend Randall Rawlings, whom he also asked to arrange for a nice day. He objected when Jackson's wife, Evelyn, née Plummer, and Scott's wife, Joanne, née Spinner, entered their names, but they told him where to place his anachronistic-chauvinistic views and got ready for the start.

"On your marks!" called the Brigadier. "Set!" His shotgun boomed, and the runners took off with young Edward Plummer in the lead. Halfway up the hill Jackson Spinner had apparently taken the lead and was going strong when he was called on by Evelyn, quite a ways back, to "wait-up, Jackson!" He kept running but then she really yelled, and he stopped. Evelyn panted up to him, took his hand and started giggling. They were then seen strolling off among the cedars, with Jackson now also giggling.

The three Plummer boys were together when they reached the top, where they were distracted by a trio of visiting young ladies from Burnaby, who were waving and taking their pictures. As the Plummers rounded the flag, Edward stopped.

"They might not be here tomorrow, boys," he said. James added, "I'm sure Tom would understand," and John said, "Hi there, girls."

Scott McConville was chugging painfully up the slope when he looked back to check on Joanne. He staggered and tripped over Windy, the Wilsons' ancient, sagging bull terrier, which had made the error of thinking it could follow young Charlie. Windy gasped, creaked and sank. Scott, ever the professional, dropped to his knees and gave the beast resuscitative measures until a breathing pattern reasserted itself, then he escorted it slowly back down the hill.

Around the first bend he found Joanne, enraptured by a pale green wood-rein orchid. She said she was off to look for more of the same.

Meanwhile, just two minutes after the race had started, Sebastian shot back across the finish line. The startled judges leaped to their feet, but Sebastian flashed by and kept on tracking. He was on a dead run for the wharf, where the *Gulf Queen*, flying in the face of history, was threatening to dock on time.

Charlie Wilson figured he must have missed his route when he looked back and ahead and saw no one else, so he took his time walking back down, where he was considerably surprised to be hailed as the winner.

"Where's the vicar?" Nelson asked, an hour later.

Reverend Rawlings appeared just as a search party was starting out. He explained that it was not often he got up the mountain and figured that when a man got that much closer to God, he should make the most of it.

Nelson has threatened to be much more choosy about who runs next year.

A Warming Trend

It had been a bad winter for power interruptions, and you could hear the groans all over the Inlet when the lights went out again on the weekend. Not that it wasn't expected; a cold westerly blow had the tallest alders straining to touch their toes. One leaned too far, barber-chaired with an explosive crack and went down in a turmoil of naked limbs and Hydro lines. The phones went out at the same time.

The Swede, just off the morning ferry after his annual week at the tables in Reno, was unpacking his couple of shirts and socks when the radio went dead. He knew some of the seniors at Pioneer Hall would need a hand if the blackout continued. The last one had gone on for three days.

He pondered whether to collect Conrad from Rachel Spinner's Derwent Kennels or to leave him another day. He thought of the old German shepherd waiting for him, and he put on his coat.

They do say it's an ill wind that blows nobody some good.

About the only communication Svensen has with Rachel is when he takes his Reno trip and leaves Conrad to be boarded. While he and Rachel are of about the same vintage—at eye-level with the old-age pension—and neither has married, they have little time for each other. Rachel believes Svensen could have left more of his logger's ways in the bunkhouse, and the Swede considers Rachel bossy.

It would be good to have Conrad back, Svensen thought, as he approached the kennels. Conrad sensed him, howled his glee and began scaling the mesh fence. In another run, one of Rachel's prize setter bitches that had recently whelped scratched fretfully at the kennel door blown shut by the wind, and whined.

Svensen turned up his coat collar against the biting cold and hammered the brass knocker on the front door. He waited, then knocked again. "She must be out," he suggested to Conrad. He checked around and realized Rachel's pickup was gone. He freed and subdued Conrad, then dropped a signed, blank cheque into Rachel's mail box.

He was turning away when the setter bitch yelped. She stared at him through the wire mesh, a plea in her liquid, intelligent eyes. She yelped again, dashed to the closed kennel door and bounced back to the fence, whining. Svensen frowned.

"Stay here," he said to Conrad, who subsided, grumbling. Inside the kennel, a row of dead heat lamps sat impotently aimed at five tiny, velvet pups huddled in a straw bed. Svensen saw one of the small bodies twitch and tremble in a fit of shivering.

Rachel Spinner fumed as the inter-islands ferry aimed its blunt bow at the Inlet dock. She'd had to go to Ganges for more feed and her stomach had twisted when the store lights flickered and died. She thought of the pups, saw in her mind the lamps fading.

She'd had to wait two hours for the ferry to leave and had watched impatiently en route as they made several attempts before finally loading a lumber truck at Otter Bay, then continuing. She gunned the pickup off the ferry and raised the eyebrows of Constable Jean LaFleur before she roared into her driveway and slammed to a stop.

The kennel door was swinging open, as was the gate to the run. The kennel was empty. Rachel pictured a prowling raccoon. Then her eye caught a flicker of light from the kitchen window. She walked cautiously along the side of the house and peered in.

Svensen was dozing before a blazing woodstove. Conrad lay at his feet. And on a scatter rug in front of the stove, bathed in a warm, red glow, the five setter pups nuzzled at their mother, who lay contentedly, one eye fixed on Svensen.

Rachel turned towards the door, then drew back. She frowned, juggling the words. "Mr. Svensen," she tried to herself. Then, "Mr. *Svensen*," and, "Mr. Svensen?"

This was not going to be easy.

Facts of Life

Samson Spinner assured the Martins that looking after their girls overnight would be a real treat. "They'll be just fine," he said.

"I know that," Sheila Martin said, as she and Paul boarded the *Gulf Queen*. "It's Samson I'm concerned for."

Samson stood looking at two gerbils, having just been advised the cage was due for a cleaning.

"Otherwithe they thtink," said the seven-year-old, Julie, a recent recipient of a cash award from the Tooth Fairy. She has Prince Valiant bangs and the eyes of a fawn, neither of which deceived Samson.

"Billy ith the one that biteth," she said now, adding, "and thatth a bad word," as Samson swore savagely and flipped one of the rat-like creatures against the cage bars until it disengaged its small, chisel teeth from the pad of flesh at the base of his forefinger. Blood welled up in beads and spilled down his hand. The girl puckered her mouth in disgust as Samson sucked the wound.

"I hope you didn't hurt him," she said accusingly.

Jillian, the nine-year-old, came in. She rolled her eyes at Samson's bloodstained paper towel.

"My dad always wears these," she said, tapping a pair of heavy leather work gloves on the window ledge. "He says he wouldn't go near the little bleepers without them."

Julie nodded. "Thatth right," she said.

They went for a drive in the afternoon and Samson bought them each a chocolate bar at Logan's store. They got back into the van while he chatted with Charlie Logan. The substantial Miss Bell-Atkinson was glaring at the van when Samson came out. The kids were chanting in crystal tones:

"Fatty, fatty, two by four,
Couldn't fit through the bathroom door;
Not too fat, not too small,
Just the size of Montreal."

Samson received from Miss Bell-Atkinson a look that should have left a scorch mark, and heard the word "degenerate" slip by his window.

"We going for beer?" Jillian asked.

Samson looked surprised. "No. Why?"

She shrugged: "Well, my mom asked my dad how much beer there was in the house and my dad said it prob'ly didn't matter how much there was because it prob'ly wouldn't be enough anyway."

They stopped once on the way back, Samson pulling gently over to the side while a doe and twin fawns crossed the dirt road.

"That," said Samson, "is the miracle of life."

"How do you get a baby in?" Julie asked him instantly, brow furrowed and eyes fixed.

"What?"

"In," she repeated firmly. "I know they come out"—she jerked her thumb at her older sister—"that one got out a year and a half before I did. But how did we get in? Like, *inthide?*" she added, in case the matter was less than clear.

They waited for his answer.

"You know," Samson said finally, "that is something I have always wondered about myself. When I find out I'll let you know." He grinned at the looks of scorn that shaped their faces.

Later, at the supper table, Jillian looked down at her plate and said, "How do they murder them?"

Samson looked at her, and at the New Zealand-born chops.

"The little white fluffy baby lambs," she continued. "These are *lamb* chops, aren't they? Off babies?"

Samson sought guidance out the window.

"They thtick a knife at them and break all their blood out," said Julie. "And their dad and mom cry."

Samson pushed the mint-jelly dish away. They ate ice cream, chips and peanut butter and watched television. The girls had their baths and then ate popcorn and nachos and drank pop while Samson lowered a can of lager.

It was very late when they went to bed, and ten minutes later little Julie padded downstairs and nudged Samson as he dozed before the television.

"I didn't get my kith," she advised.

He gave her one, smelling the soap and warmth and honey-breath, and chuckled.

"No problem at all," he told Sheila Martin brightly when she came off the ferry the next day.

"Let me know if you get stuck again . . . like, really stuck."

Brothers

Samson Spinner watched sympathetically as Angus Turner left the Cedars, his thin shoulders bowed.

"Poor old bugger," he murmured.

Angus has cultivated adversity since he got off the boat in Montreal in 1946, a fresh-faced 21-year-old from Aberdeen. His military service had consisted of three years of writing press releases about the war effort at home. He has worked for newspapers in more small towns across Canada than he cares to recall.

In the early days, each job would go well for a while, and Angus would be eyed for promotion. Then there'd be the occasional missed day, and the clues in the watery red eyes. And then it would be a missed week, and the fuzzy recollections. And then the knowing and sad shake of the head, and the pink slip. To his mother, and his brother in England, he wrote irregularly, and always in bursts of optimism. Each town was a greater opportunity, another step to success. They replied at increasingly longer intervals.

Angus's last job was as a low-level public relations man where only his ability to bang out a crisp news release at short notice kept him long enough to collect a token pension before his thirst once more caught up with him. He lives rent-free in a small cabin and watches over the property of an Arizona oil man. He occasionally writes a small piece for Elliott Smalley at *The Tidal Times*. When he submerges for a few days, an eye is kept on him.

"His brother became a heavy-duty lawyer and then judge in the old country," Samson told Nelson Spinner. "They pretty well lost contact. Now the brother is in Seattle for a justice seminar and he's coming to see Angus for the weekend. I've never seen Angus so down."

Nelson ordered a couple more beer.

Later, Samson drove a nervous Angus to the ferry in Chief Jimmy Plummer's new Oldsmobile. Angus had dressed carefully and trimmed his hair. He kept putting his ragged fingernails out of sight.

The *Gulf Queen* docked, and Andrew Turner strode off, an impeccably dressed, dignified gentleman. His eyes, bright and quizzical, touched on Angus, flickered away, then came back and rested. A small, thoughtful frown touched his face, and left. He smiled.

"Angus!" he said.

Samson Spinner shook Andrew Turner's hand, then waved him to the car. On the back seat lay a copy of *The Tidal Times* with a page-one Angus Turner byline in the biggest type Elliott had used since the Queen waved at the Inlet from the royal yacht. Under the byline, it said "Associate Editor."

On the way to the oil man's property, they made several stops to introduce Andrew. At each, Angus was greeted with considerably more enthusiasm than he is accustomed to. At the oil man's house, Angus led his brother to the guest suite.

"I've never seen such a place, Angus," his brother said. Angus poured drinks.

Samson was around most of the weekend, seeing that they kept on the go, and interrupting conversations that might get too deep into the past. He skippered the oil man's cruiser when they went fishing, and chauffeured the Jeep on an island tour.

Angus passed airily over questions about his career as the brothers sat at breakfast on the last morning. "Oh, most of the big papers," he said, not quite holding his brother's eye. "Correspondent, columnist, editor . . . finally reached the point where every story seemed to be a re-run. So I quit. And here I am." He waved his hand at the rich furnishings and the clear-cedar panelling.

Andrew nodded. "I'm very happy for you, Angus. I always thought you would do well, and so you have."

At the ferry, the brothers embraced, and a small tear slipped down Andrew's face. He shook hands with Samson, and held his eyes. And with a small smile, he said, "I've always maintained, Mr. Spinner, that good friends are at least as valuable as great riches."

He nodded, looking at Angus a few steps away.

"I can see that my brother has become a very wealthy man," he said. "And I thank all of you for that."

The Expert Touch

"You should let somebody do it who knows how," said Svensen, shifting a chaw around with his tongue. "An expert."

Lennie Wilson snorted as he craned his neck to look up the length of the fir. "I've taken trees down before, Svensen—drop it on a dime if I want."

The old logger grunted.

Maggie had advised Lennie she was spending no more summers with a sun-deck that lived in perpetual shade, so would he please remove some of the offenders. Lennie started his saw, goosed it, and began the undercut. He went low on one side and, after some hacking and cursing, popped out a wedge that lacked something in symmetry. Svensen winced.

Lennie scowled and spat on his hands, then stood back and lined up the tree. "Here she goes, then," he said. The chain bit in and the fir began to waver and turn on the uneven undercut.

"Christ!" Lennie observed, and leaped back.

The fir toppled, wheeling gently as it fell. It scraped the side of the house and put an end to Windy's kennel. The Wilson's geriatric bull terrier, likely with some sense of events, was off in the bush offering challenges to the goat.

Maggie appeared on the back porch, her dark Spanish eyes flashing. "I would like to keep the house," she said.

Svensen snorted and Lennie turned on him. "Shut up or bugger off," he said. And to Maggie, "A tiny error, my darling."

He let the Swede help him buck the fir up and clear the branches. Then he turned on a sturdy hemlock that had been denying Maggie the full benefits of the setting sun. His undercut was perfect this time. Svensen made as if to offer a comment, but Lennie's sharply raised warning finger stopped him.

The hemlock fell straight as a fainting guardsman. It was while the tree was gathering speed that Lennie realized he had gravely underestimated its height.

Lennie's property adjoins that of the Reverend Randall Rawlings, who was watching Lennie at work from his study window, and admiring the new cedar fence that Sebastian Whittle had just completed around the rectory.

The Reverend Rawlings' mouth opened but his small cry of distress was lost in the crash of the hemlock landing on the fence and leaving three sections of it flat and in splinters. He made a move as though immediately to go and discuss the damage with Lennie, but postponed it as Lennie began graphically describing the tree, its antecedents, and their collective shortcomings.

"Don't say nothin', Svensen," Lennie warned. The Swede nodded and again helped buck and clear.

There was one large alder to go. Lennie sharpened the chain, spat on his hands and rubbed them together. He backed off, eyed the tree carefully, then paced off a distance in a clear area up past the woodshed, stood, and took several deep breaths.

Then he shook his head, muttered, "Ah the hell with it," and pointed to the Swede, then to the saw. Svensen nodded, smiled, and hefted the saw. He made a swift undercut and the wedge came out like a butter pat.

Some alders grow with a built-in twist, almost a spiral. They look straight, but inside is a contained warp, a collection of pent-up energy and tension just begging for release. The bite of a chainsaw can do it, at which moment the true soul of the tree explodes from its bonds, into the shape it always wanted, and tears itself apart.

This one did just that, splitting with a thundering crack to halfway up its length from the Swede's saw cut. One piece lashed past Lennie's face, its lethal whisper turning him pale, and then the whole thing groaned, twisted, and toppled in precisely the opposite direction the Swede had intended. Svensen had long fled the spot, the first tell-tale cracking of the strained fibres lending a quick knowledge and remarkable nimbleness to his elderly legs.

The tree spiralled, caressed the house's east gable, then spun away and deftly took out Maggie's washing, the Hydro and phone lines and one complete power pole, before landing with a shuddering thud, dead-centre in the driveway. The earth trembled, and rested. There was a lengthy silence while Lennie and the Swede observed the tangle of bedsheets, wires, limbs and pole.

Finally Lennie chuckled, and then he laughed. "It's a good job we had an expert on that one, Svensen," he said. "We could have had ourselves a hell of a mess."

The Right Spirit

Elliott Smalley rolled his eyes and finally agreed to write something about the Spinner's Inlet Psychic Society. "But I'll make it clear it's your idea, not mine," he admonished Barbara Spinner.

"Nothing better to do with their time," he grumbled, as Barbara left. "Creepy lot," he added.

It was just then that he saw Fred Cannonby hunched over the old Underwood at the corner desk. But the Underwood had gone years ago, and Fred was writing speeches in Ottawa the last time Elliott heard. Elliott blinked and Fred was gone. The desk as usual held the office's one video display terminal.

"It's the spiritualists," he told himself. "They're getting to you."

He went back to the paste-up board and was just sizing a picture of the school volleyball team when he clearly heard Fred Cannonby's voice saying, "Crop that tighter, Elliott."

He jumped, and turned around. Of course, the office was empty. The voice had been as grumpy as ever. Fred had worked on the Vancouver dailies and had taught Elliott most of what he knew about the newspaper business. He was usually blunt, often impatient, and always right. "Don't tell me about it," he would snap. "Write it!"

Elliott swore quietly after Barbara Spinner. "Witches," he muttered. Then he studied the picture, frowned, looked over his shoulder, and quickly cropped out an errant nose and chin on the left.

He tidied up and prepared to leave, as he had promised Barbara he would take in one meeting of the society. "Just to get the flavour of it," she'd said.

Elliott picked up his coat, and stopped. There was something nagging him about the page he'd just laid out. He went back to it and his eyes locked on a headline he'd written in a hurry:

Boomers win with

Wilson in the net

He had a picture in his mind of Fred Cannonby's fat blue editing pencil angrily ripping through typescript, paper and all, as he advised Elliott, "Don't end a line in a head with a bloody preposition!" Elliott circled the "with" for correction, and froze as Fred Cannonby grunted, "Thank you." He shut the door behind him quickly.

Elliott was prepared for the worst at the Spinner home: smoke, mirrors and black cats. Instead, the group was sitting around sipping tea in the living room and smiled happily when Elliott joined them: Barbara, Melinda Spinner, Mrs. Brigadier, and Thelma Spooner. There was no fuss. They simply went quiet when Melinda put her teacup down rather sharply and sat up.

"It's Great-Aunt Annabel again," she said, her head cocked.

The others nodded. Annabel Spinner had been the only daughter of three children of the patriarch Samson Spinner. She had remained a spinster and at the age of 56, in 1911, was lost in the tragic sinking of the S.S. Iroquois in a storm off Sidney. She is said to have been a frequent visitor since.

"She's pointing to Elliott," Melinda said.

"She would be," Elliott thought sarcastically.

"She says there's somebody . . . can't get the name . . . telling Elliott the picture looks much better. I think the name is . . . Ned?"

"Fred," said Elliott, putting his cup down with a clatter.

"That's it," Melinda said.

Elliott left and went to *The Tidal Times* office, where the phone was ringing. The call was from Vancouver.

"Yeah, it's a shock, all right, Elliott. We just got word. Sudden, at the National Press Club, apparently . . . glass in hand, of course— good a way to go as any, I guess. Yeah, we're organizing a wake. Poor old Fred, eh?"

Later Elliott sat at the video display terminal and typed:

"One of the more intriguing groups in the Inlet . . . "

He stopped and looked around. He could have sworn he'd heard a familiar chuckle.

Old Soldiers

The Brigadier was back from a brief pilgrimage to the beach at Normandy where 40 years ago he had led a company of frightened men, some of whom did not return. His eyes were bright as he described the trip to Chief Jimmy Plummer over a drink at the Legion.

At the next table the Plummer boys exchanged "Oh-God" glances as the pair of older men slipped into reminiscences. Chief Jimmy was not at Normandy, but he has acute memories of snow-swept valleys and bleak, blasted slopes in Korea.

"That's when I really understood the expression 'waves of people'," he said. "I couldn't see how we'd ever get out."

He'd been one of the four in his platoon who did get out on that occasion. And he did it carrying a young second lieutenant from the Princess Pats across his shoulder, for which he owns, kept in a small box among his socks and underwear, the George Cross.

Young Edward Plummer, recently of drinking age, and cocky, groaned aloud as Chief Jimmy continued.

That was on Friday. The day after, Chief Jimmy had to go into Vancouver and he invited Edward along.

"Where are we going?" Edward asked as they turned off Oak Street.

"See a coupla people." Chief Jimmy swung into the hospital parking lot. "Down here." He nodded along the green and beige corridor. Edward's nose wrinkled at the smells of the old and permanently ill.

They stopped outside a big room where a dozen or so patients sat around large tables. Most of them were old men in wheelchairs. Some were knitting, their faces wrinkled with concentration; some frowned as they fitted puzzle blocks together.

Edward's eyes fixed on one old man with white hair cropped close to his skull. He was holding a skein of wool stretched between what had once been large, strong hands; now they were mottled parchment over bone. A nurse stood in front of his wheelchair, rolling the wool into a ball and good-humouredly chiding him when the loop slipped from his hands and tangled, which it did often. A tear welled up at intervals in the old man's eyes and slipped down his cheek. He had two shiny medals hanging from rich-hued ribbons pinned to his pyjama jacket.

A young girl of about eight turned and bumped into Edward, and apologized. She was with a grey-haired woman who sat in a chair in a small alcove, the back of her head resting against the wall, her eyes closed.

The woman held the hand of a slim, upright man who sat in a wheelchair under the window, his legs covered by a grey blanket. His eyes rested on something a distance away. He had been a handsome man once, years ago, before the damage to the left side of his face, which was now crumpled and oddly shiny. He wore a faded shoulder flash stitched to his pyjama pocket: Canadian Scottish.

The little girl was talking to him. "I'll make you some cookies, grandpa. I got a dog as well—you'll like him. I wanted to bring him to visit but I don't think they 'low pets."

She turned to the grey-haired woman.

"He's listening, sweetheart. He knows what you're saying," the woman said. She raised herself from the chair as a nurse approached, and she patted the man's hand.

"We'll see you next week," she said as the nurse wheeled him away. She caught Chief Jimmy's eyes as she turned to leave, and smiled.

"He has some good days," she said. The thoughts in her eyes

shifted. "And we had some good years before he went like this. That's more than a lot of them got, isn't it?"

She took the child's hand and they trudged off.

Edward was quiet for the rest of the afternoon while Chief Jimmy got his business finished and they headed back for the ferry. They called in at the Legion for a quick beer on the way home. The Brigadier was at a corner table with Nelson Spinner.

"I'll get them," Edward told his father, and went to the bar.

He returned to the table with four drinks, including the Brigadier's brandy and ginger ale. He pulled up a chair next to the Brigadier., Chief Jimmy's face was impassive as Edward turned to the old soldier during a lull in the conversation.

"I was wondering," Edward said. "How many of the fellows you knew back then were in France this time . . . ?"

Verse and Worse

A couple of times a year, Elliott Smalley comes up with a competition in *The Tidal Times*. This time it was limericks with BC place names or themes.

First prize was a year's subscription. Elliott ignored Lennie Wilson's suggestion that the second prize should be two years' subscription. He also rejected out of hand Lennie's first submission, a dreadfully lewd thing about the farmyard adventures of a young lady from Choate.

Elliott gave special mention to the Swede's entry, declaring it a fine example of the pithiness of both the logging fraternity and of someone who'd had to overcome the obstacle of learning a second language. Svensen figured there was little profit in advising Elliott that he had been born and raised in Chilliwack. The Swede wrote:

Two loggers on one BC Ferry
Were making excessively merry.
One fell in the chuck.
When his partner called, "Buck,
Is it cold?" He said, "Very."

There was one anonymous one that Elliott ran, thinking that it was written on the kind of notepaper he had seen in the study of the Reverend Randall Rawlings.

A daring young woman from Hope
Made a telephone call to the Pope.
The Vatican said
"He has just gone to bed."
"Can't you raise him?" She asked.
They said, "Nope."

Elliott quite enjoyed giving prominence to the one from Evelyn Spinner, it coming just after Evelyn and Jackson had had a relatively minor but very audible dispute down at the marina.

"A Warning To Overbearing Husbands", he titled it:

A fellow who lived out in Delta
Was rough on his wife, he would belta
Around and around
But one day he was found,
Stuffed into a smelta in Delta.

He put a signs-of-the-times sub-head over Chief Jimmy Plummer's entry. Chief Jimmy had just returned from visiting relatives in the interior, and wrote:

A rancher from up Kamloops way
Said, "I've had a hell of a day;
"My sons can't ride horses,
"My girl's joined the forces,
"And three of my cowboys are gay."

He ran the two Martin girls' pieces side by side in a wide-ruled box, with a note that he was awarding them each a five-dollar "special merit" prize. The little one, Julie, wrote:

A girl who lived in Bella Bella
Was seen with a very strange fella;
His navel, you see,
Was below his left knee,
And his three eyes were red, blue and yella.

And Jillian came up with:

There was a young woman from Lytton
Who one day got quite badly bytton
By several black ants
That crept in her pants.
"They got me," she said, "Where I sytton."

Elliott remarked that they had no doubt got their talent from their classics-educated teacher mother, not their father, whose contribution ran alongside:

There was a young maiden from Lumby
Who complained of a pain in her tumby.
The doctor said "Well,
"While it's early to tell,
"I think you'll soon be a mumby!"

The Brigadier surprised everyone and took the seniors' class award with:

A lady in Likely, once told,
By a fellow exceedingly bold,
That, if she didn't mind,
He would pinch her behind,
Said, "Not likely! But wait—
Oh, all right, then, grab hold!"

Elliott was well aware that criticism would be his lot no matter what he selected as the grand winner, so he went with the one that tickled him most. It was Lennie's second entry:

There was a young lady from Spuzzum,

Who had a great pride in her buzzum.
But one day in December
She forgot to remember
To cover them up, and she fruzzum.

Double Fault

Froelich has made almost an obsession of ignoring the Slaters since the well-drilling incident. His refusal to consider a water-rental arrangement with Jason Slater pushed the young musician into costly drilling, and resulted in Froelich's water supply being tapped and significantly reduced. He has since refused to acknowledge the Slaters' existence.

He scowled now as he straightened up from the string levels he was laying and glanced up the neighbour's slope, where fresh pegs hung with fluttering orange tape marked the foundation corners of the Slaters' weekend cottage.

Then his face relaxed as he stood back and visualized his new tennis court. The chain-link fence would end perfectly, right there, if he removed just five sections of the old board structure separating the properties. That would leave enough room for a nice flagstone path on the other side, between the new court and the pool. And he could fasten canvas high up against the chain-link, and that would block out the Slaters.

His scowl reappeared when he saw Jason approaching him down the field, waving.

"Mr. Froelich! I'd like to speak to you!"

Froelich gave a quick, dismissive wave of his hand, and stamped off into the house. Jason had started to climb the fence, but he lowered himself back down. "I'll phone him," he said.

He did, and Froelich slammed the phone down after barking out, "Don't talk to me, you hear!"

And to his wife he growled, "No snotty-nosed kids are getting on my tennis court." She said maybe that wasn't what Jason wanted, but Froelich said of course it was, so she let it be.

Froelich's place, with its big pool and high fences, is known casually in the Inlet as The Country Club. Not that any of the locals have a membership. While he talks loudly enough about his pool and cabanas and, lately, his planned tennis court, he reserves their comforts for the occasional visits by cronies from the prairies.

Jason wrote two letters and dropped them in Froelich's mail box, one marked "Important We Talk," the other, "LISTEN!" He found them both, unopened, nailed to the forms where the foundations of his new house were being poured.

Jason was standing outside Logan's store explaining things to Nelson Spinner when Froelich drove past. Jason tried to flag him down but Froelich stared ahead and kept going. The day before, the crew from Vancouver had arrived while the Slaters were away and prepared the foundation for the tennis court.

Nelson Spinner shrugged. "You might as well discuss it with that hemlock over there if Froelich's dug his heels in," he said. "Tennis, anyone?" he added.

Later, Jason looked down the slope toward Froelich's place and shook his head. The fresh blacktop shone and the white markings reflected the morning sun. The chain-link fence stood on guard for Froelich. A roll of heavy green canvas lay at the side facing the Slaters.

Froelich stood behind the mesh, hands on hips, watching. He didn't move as Jason walked down the slight incline and up to him. They faced each other through the open mesh and Jason opened his mouth to speak.

Froelich anticipated him. "You had something to say?" he asked, with his thin smile.

Jason nodded. "I did, but you wouldn't let me," he said. "I had the property surveyed before we put the house stakes in." He pointed to the ancient board fence. "That," he said, "and about 15 inches of your new tennis court, is on my property."

He started to walk away, then turned. "Your serve," he said.

Back in the Saddle

It was painfully clear that young Heather Spooner's reach had exceeded her grasp by a considerable margin when she officially opened her riding club last week. The fence around the ring was incomplete, like a dozen other things, and as her mother, Thelma, told her, she should have postponed the event. The bubbling impatience of youth ruled, however, and the result was that the youngster was in danger of being gravely embarrassed in front of the whole community—and especially Miss Bell-Atkinson.

Miss Bell-Atkinson closed the original Equestrian Academy ten years ago, and Heather's is the first serious attempt to replace it.

Miss Bell-Atkinson was among the early arrivals, placing herself at one end of the half-fenced ring where she had an overview of the unfolding calamities. Even those who came to lend encouragement and help, despite their good intentions, became part of the problem.

Constable Jean LaFleur, for example, provided quite eloquent proof of why he had never made the short list for the musical ride during his time at the academy in Regina. Miss Bell-Atkinson simply closed her eyes tightly as the young Mountie concluded a ragged trot around the ring on the dun pony Heather had allotted him, by sliding—as the pony halted suddenly and lowered its head into a bucket—inexorably forward and down over the animal's neck and head, and landing hands first in what was the rich beginning of a supply of agricultural nutrient.

As the policeman made a familiar and accurate observation in French, Heather's face tightened, but she forced a smile to meet the rising laughter coming from the sidelines.

Samson Spinner had meant to do particularly well for Heather, given his growing interest in her mother, who is a most attractive and youngish widow. But as a horseman he lacks the right stuff. Miss Bell-Atkinson watched him with undisguised disdain as he arrived, protectively geared-out in bright yellow hard hat and standard work boots.

"Is he planning to ride the beast, or build it a home?" she was heard to mutter.

Heather put him aboard Gentle George, a torpid bay gelding. Samson enjoyed the initial moments as the horse ambled off among the tall cedars, became a little concerned when it broke into a lumbering and uncharacteristic trot, and fell off after a whack in the hard hat from a skulking bough that rang his bells for half an hour afterwards. This was comical, as testified by Lennie Wilson's braying laughter.

Heather's face lengthened, and her bright young eyes became bleak. It was becoming one of those situations where the more everyone tried to help, the worse it was, and Heather's hopes seemed to be headed for the trampled straw and mud of the unfinished ring. Everyone could see what was happening, and no one seemed to be able to stop it.

Except one.

Miss Bell-Atkinson suddenly rose from her place and, her impeccably-tailored hacking jacket and tweed skirt lending an astonished dignity to the moment, stalked to the small microphone that Heather had set up to announce the lamentable proceedings.

"Not bad!" Her booming syllables sent birds crashing through the foliage and up into the blue.

"For a dress rehearsal," she added. "We all know about dress rehearsals, don't we?" No one disagreed. "If the rough edges show then, the opening will be stunning. That's tomorrow of course," she added, "starting at the same time."

That was news to everybody, including Heather who had the good sense to stay silent.

Miss Bell-Atkinson's eyes fixed on Samson. "Mr. Spinner, a word," she said. "And Mr. Wilson." She stared past their shoulders as she talked intently at them, turning frequently to nod her head toward Heather.

The next morning the ring was complete with a white-painted rail fence, carpeted in fresh sawdust and bedecked with a grand assortment of flags. Red and blue barrels supported gleaming jumping poles.

At noon, with the crowd triple what it had been the day before, Heather placed a record on the turntable and the sound of the "William Tell" overture cut the air.

There was a clatter from the stable area and Miss Bell-Atkinson rode into the ring on a beautifully proportioned young grey mare and sailed effortlessly over a tricky series of Calvaletti jumps. Even Samson and Lennie put down their paintbrushes and cans to join in the spontaneous applause.

Miss Bell-Atkinson dismounted, handed the reins to Heather and placed an arm around the girl's shoulders. "Good luck, my dear," she said.

The smile on the youngster's face was something to see.

Out of Line

The clerk behind the counter caught Rachel Spinner's eye, read her thoughts, and shrugged sympathetically. Rachel was at the back of the long lineup for renewing drivers' licences.

Rachel detests lineups. "Just another theft of time," she says. She tapped one foot as the licence line stirred but failed to advance.

The drive in from the ferry hadn't helped, with the tunnel traffic jammed back up to the Ladner overpass and lunatics cutting in to gain a car length. She had rolled her window down and preferred a searing critique against one young culprit in a convertible who finished up next to her. His ears turned crimson and his eyes widened as Rachel gave him a quick character rundown. A trucker in the third lane had listened, nodded admiringly, and said, "Wonderful, that was."

A child whined while it kicked at a soft-drink machine at the end of the motor vehicle branch office. It rattled the machine's swivel door and stabbed the coin-release button. The child's mother stood at the end of the lineup for new licences and road tests, a long cigarette attached to the corner of her mouth. "Stop it, Aaron," she said. The child ignored her and battered the machine.

The mother picked at old vermilion polish on her fingernails and squinted against a rising fan of cigarette smoke. She was directly under a small, hand-lettered sign that requested no smoking, if you would be so kind. She caught Rachel's eyes drilling her, watched them move from her to the boy whose nose now was running copiously as he continued kicking the machine, and resumed her quiescent stance.

"Colour of eyes?" The clerk's voice rose slightly over the restless hum.

"Brown," answered the tall blonde woman at the head of Rachel's line.

"Hair?" he continued mechanically.

"Can't you see?" the woman snapped.

The clerk's shoulders sagged just slightly, then he looked up. "Blonde," he said writing. And added softly, "Today."

Rachel snorted and the man looked up and a dry little smile touched his lips and slipped away. Then his eyes dulled and his brow creased as the snotty-nosed child screamed at the machine and yelled, "Pop! I wan' pop!" at its mother.

The clerk, a man with grey, thinning hair and gold-rimmed glasses, said, as though to himself, "No, child, that is not what you want," and he examined the mother, who blew smoke and stared sourly back at him.

The blonde woman wouldn't place her feet in the footprints drawn in felt pen on the tile floor, the positioning for the camera. "I look terrible from that side!" she snapped. And she argued with him over removing her glasses for the photo, while he patiently explained that it is a law-enforcement requirement, because large spectacles often hide facial features.

As she left, she told him she was sick of bloody civil servants who got paid for sitting around on their arses and taking coffee breaks, running her life. The clerk removed his glasses and rubbed his eyes. He looked at his wristwatch as the next person moved up.

The child punched its mother and shouted for pop and the mother lit a cigarette from the butt of the last one and said, "Stop it, Aaron."

Rachel's turn came. He wanted her height and weight—in metric.

Rachel flared. "I'm five foot one and three quarters, and I weigh... ah... 112 pounds," she said, blushing slightly.

He studied her for a second, and the little grin came.

"Well, for converting, let's just round it out at five foot two and 110 pounds," he said. "How's that?"

They cleared the rest quickly, including her mother's maiden name —the licence-security device—which was whispered around the corner of the counter.

As Rachel moved to leave, she saw the clerk examine the lineup behind her, which had doubled in length. Half-way down it, a couple in garish punk regalia argued in loud and vulgar terms. The child banged fiercely against the drink machine, and yelled.

Rachel made for the door, then stopped. She turned and walked up to the child.

"Stop it, and shut up!" The voice was a whipcrack, and the result was a power cut. The child's mouth hung open, silent. There were murmurs of approval from the lines of waiting.

Rachel turned to the mother.

"Wipe his nose," she said. And added, "And put that damned cigarette out!" There were several cries of "All right!" as Rachel swept out, but Rachel enjoyed most the smile on the face of the grey-haired clerk.

Arts and Craft

"That writer's coming back," Samson Spinner told Nelson as they sat at the Cedars combining cider and Guinness into wholesome Black Velvets. "He says this time he would like to see the 'truly creative element' of the community, do a series of vignettes on the 'artistes' of the island."

The year before, the magazine writer had spent two days in the Inlet, was given the royal treatment, and enraged the community by writing a simpering piece about Singlestar and his band of "Lost Children of the '60s," who are actually a bunch of unwashed delinquents who collect social assistance and squat on a patch of Crown land.

Nelson carefully wiped the foam from his top lip. "I think we should help the man," he said.

Samson met the writer off the Saturday-morning ferry.

"Wonderful!" the visitor gushed. "Such characters!" as Lennie Wilson, minus his dentures and wearing his decaying naval cap back to front, stuck his head through the side window and recited a sibilant, clumsily rhyming quatrain of astounding vulgarity.

"A poet of the fundamental school," Samson said. "He's applying for a Canada Council grant."

"Very, very earthy stuff," the writer nodded, scribbling in his notebook.

Samson parked the van at the end of Ennerdale Road and signalled the writer to go quietly as they stepped onto a bush trail. They stopped where it opened out onto the banks of Gilgarren Creek. A figure in a flowing smock and stained red beret stood, palette and brush in hand, staring raptly at a half-finished canvas.

"He has been compared to the mature Goya," Samson whispered, as Nelson swung round and glared at them from slightly maddened eyes, then turned back to his canvas.

"Note the passion, the bold declaration of the human condition," Samson recited. "The, ah . . . " he glanced down at a small card folded in his palm, "the petty and ignoble vices . . . and yet the compassion, too."

The writer nodded and stepped forward, then retreated as Nelson spun and again turned his demented look on them, his lips twitching. Samson could just discern the outline of the paint-by-numbers set on the canvas and noticed that the human form taking shape bore a remarkable similarity to the jovial Green Giant of vegetable advertising fame.

"We intrude," Samson whispered. His voice trembled and he appeared to shudder as he led the writer back to the van. Minutes later they pulled up at the post office.

"Wait 'til you hear this," Samson said.

Thelma Spooner smiled as they entered. At Samson's nod she struck a pose and launched into a screeching version of "O Sole Mio." The effect was not unlike that of someone dragging a sharp spike down a long tin roof.

Thelma's terrier left abruptly by the back door, while outside a cheep of chickadees shot away in startled concert from the branches of a small elderberry tree. Thelma held a long, last grating note and Samson shouted "Bravo!" several times. She gargled to a halt and smiled ingratiatingly at the writer, whose face was engraved in a kind of wonder.

"She auditioned for the CBC," Samson advised. The writer nodded. "They said they would let her know," Samson added.

The writer was quiet as Samson turned into the Plummers' yard. Chief Jimmy was standing between two saw-horses, banging away at a slim pole with a small hatchet.

"The chief's carvings are as yet little known," Samson observed. "But we expect that one day his name will be inscribed alongside those of the great."

"I thought they used cedar logs," the writer said.

"The chief likes the challenge of a simple piece of alder," Samson explained. He gestured to about three cords of split firewood sitting under a lean-to. "As you see, there is a lot of trial and error involved."

Lennie was at the wharf again when they went for the night ferry, doing his primitive nose-and-mouth, one-man-band act for a line of awed foot passengers.

"A veritable treasury of talent," Samson said reverently.

The ferry arrived and the writer prepared to board.

"So when can we expect to read your piece?" Samson asked.

The writer looked up at him for some moments, then, through his furrowed expression a tiny light flickered.

"I think," he said "we might wait until Mrs. Spooner hears back from the CBC."

Two of a Kind

The fire hazard was extreme all summer and almost everyone had been extra cautious. Froelich, of course, does what suits him. Like a few others.

Although Froelich took up a token stance with his garden hose while he burned a stack of rubbish, the inevitable happened. A small cedar shaving, glowing red, rose like a feather on an updraft and climbed and drifted.

Still glowing, it settled some distance away on the resting bum of Miss Bell-Atkinson's superannuated basset hound, Sarah. Sarah grunted at the first touch, and almost rose. The ember burned through hair and settled on skin. Sarah howled, came upright, accelerated to a full trundle, and plunged out onto the road—where she narrowly missed a hammering from the front shoes of Heather Spooner's little palomino.

The horse shied, skittered and sidestepped into the path of a heads-down cyclist whose equipment had been loaded with more ambition than skill and who screamed, wobbled and careered off into the bushes.

It was agreed later that sympathy for the youth was misplaced, when Sebastian Whittle from the ferry booth identified him as the leader of a clutter of cyclists who that morning had shouted a collective rudeness when asked to let the cars leave the ferry first and who continued defiantly riding the yellow line until Constable Jean LaFleur shaped them up.

The sympathy came from Heather, and from Miss Bell-Atkinson who apologized for Sarah's unlikely and unexplained burst of motion. The cyclist took it with poor grace and left grumbling and with his head down again—which was his second oversight in about as many minutes, because, had he been looking up, he would have seen the Brigadier who, in his Mini-minor, also has an affinity for the yellow centre line.

In avoiding the Brigadier, and accompanied by the Brigadier's reverberating and aspersive opinions on his parentage and his probable intellectual boundaries, the cyclist hung a sharp left, which took him at a quick and wobbly clip down the slope to Jackson Spinner's marina.

His arrival there was abrupt and untidy and he was prevented from entering the chilly waters of Spinner's Inlet only by the intervention of a heavy and well-tarred dock piling, its tar softening in the afternoon sun, with which he found himself in close embrace.

"All he needs now is feathers," remarked Sebastian, who was spending an idle hour interrupting Jackson's work, and who viewed the cyclist's unusual arrival and current condition as a happy form of retribution, given the youth's earlier behaviour.

Froelich, who had come down to admire the lines of his new cabin cruiser, and to whom the misfortune of others is prime entertainment, laughed uproariously at Sebastian's sally. Froelich's braying apparently snapped the cyclist's already rather-tightened tolerance of what he saw as a day of acute persecution. The youth made a fast and decidedly threatening move.

Froelich, a practised survivor, effected a judicious sidestep; or, it would have been—had the move not caused him to trip on the eight-by-eight secured to the dock's edge and spin gracefully over and into the Inlet. The event seemed to satisfy the cyclist, who chortled as Froelich, spluttering and adorned with various marine plants, heaved himself back onto the dock.

"Serves you bloody right," the youth observed.

Which, in light of the day's events, seemed to be a fair summation.

A Log of Love

Samson Spinner was out of the van in short order when he saw the surveyor's ribbon fluttering from a spike in the wedding tree. There was a long line of ribbons on various trees stretching off down Ennerdale Road.

A highways department truck from Victoria pulled up nearby and a foreman climbed out with papers and a lunch bucket under his arm. The big maple was in the path of a road-widening project, the foreman explained. It was going to have to come down.

Samson laughed and shook his head. "Not that one," he said. "That one's part of the family. Come here."

The foreman followed Samson up to the tree and had his attention drawn to several sets of deeply carved initials on various parts of the ancient, gnarled trunk. Some of them were distorted and almost buried by the bark that had grown around them. There's hardly a pioneer family in Spinner's Inlet that doesn't have a record of a marriage performed under the big tree, in the years before a church was built. Nor, Samson mused, one without a history of passions consummated somewhere in the shade of its great, spreading canopy.

The tree was old when his own great-grandfather, Paul Spinner, the first of the line born in the Inlet, placed a simple gold band on the finger of Caroline Nelson on a sunny Easter weekend in 1879.

The foreman shrugged, and tapped a large-scale map. "It's on the righta-way, pal."

He had his orders, he said, and the way things are with government jobs these days, he wasn't about to argue with them. The crew would be here in a couple of days, he said.

At a full meeting of the Spinner and Plummer families later, Samson reported: "I phoned the provincial government heritage people. The lady was very nice but she said she's afraid they don't do trees. She said that would be up to the local government."

"It's a pity we don't have one," said his father, Wilson Spinner.

"It is that," agreed Chief Jimmy Plummer.

The road crew arrived on the Wednesday morning, and stood nonplussed but grinning at the scene around the big maple. Samson, in morning coat and grey topper, his usually unruly curls suitably trimmed, stood upright beside Thelma Spooner, who appeared to have been lovingly poured into an ivory-silk wedding gown that shimmered in the early sun. The Reverend Randall Rawlings smiled down at the pair and around at the wedding party of about 50 people. The road crew watched and smiled as Samson lifted Thelma's hand then turned and kissed her fully and at some length. The Reverend Rawlings finally harrumphed at them to quit it.

A small choir, in full cassocks and surplices, and accompanied by young Charlie Wilson on his flute, sang softly, "All You Need Is Love."

Silver and crystal sat on pure white linen on tables arranged around the tree. The road crew were beckoned and ushered gently but firmly into seats and immediately became part of the celebration, where the first and many of the subsequent courses seemed to come out of champagne bottles.

The crew joined in the long and loud applause as Samson took a heavy hunting knife and carved his and Thelma's initials, and the date, into the maple's crusted bark. Thelma later remarked that it was nice for a girl to have something in writing, anyway.

The Reverend Rawlings, studying a passing cloud, quietly reminded Samson that it was the practice for actual weddings to follow rehearsals within a reasonable time. Samson said he certainly would bear that in mind.

The road-widening job is now finished. As you come around the corner on Ennerdale Road there's a splendid new sweep of blacktop. It divides just before it reaches the big maple and forms a neatly curving lane on each side of the old tree before joining up again a little farther along.

The vicar is taking reservations for wedding services under the tree.

Show Horse

The five kids from the Spinner's Inlet Riding Club were working hard at the old stiff-upper-lip routine, but it was tough going.

"We're going to get wiped," observed young Julie Martin as she fed apple bits to Snappy, the fat and sometimes fractious Shetland pony.

"Oh, ye of little faith," responded Sally Rawlings, the eldest of the Reverend Randall and Kitty Rawlings' brood. "But you're right, kid," she added.

And yet everything had started so well. They'd all been bubbling with excitement when they left the Inlet aboard the ferry with the shouts of well-wishers in their wake. Snappy and Platonica, the little bay mare, had co-operated when loaded into the back of Heather Spooner's truck, rubbing up against each other with obvious pleasure and letting fly at the raised tailgate only once as the truck rattled on board.

The trip up the valley had included a stop at the Cloverdale McDonald's where the kids had stuffed themselves almost comatose. And the night under canvas in the horse-show field had been a delight of stories in the dark and outbursts of giggling, with little Willie Whittle, Sebastian's youngest, and the only male in the group, advising them that this trip had proved, if nothing else, that all girls were permanently out to lunch.

It was the appearance next morning of their competition that threatened to knock their socks off. As they emerged from the tent, a large man dressed in hunting pink and all the trimmings had stared down from the saddle of a monstrous and improbably glossy thoroughbred with exquisitely braided tail and mane, and advised them they were in the path of arriving equestrians, and on private property.

Heather's explanation that they were competitors in the day's equitation cast a glaze over the man's eyes which was in no way lessened when his gaze alighted on Snappy and Platonica, each of whom is some lengths removed from the thoroughbred line and whose coats were at that moment not so much glossy as kind of quilted-looking and covered with bits of hay and clover.

They looked much sharper when groomed and saddled, with ribbons in their manes, and the kids were outfitted about as smartly as anyone in the show. Nevertheless, young Julie's words had the ring of truth.

Each of the five had already placed either last or next-to-last in separate events, and despite the sincere applause the crowd came up with for them, they couldn't help but feel they had ventured a bit beyond their station. They might have gone completely squelched, but for Platonica's wonky knee and the big thoroughbred's lusty inclinations.

They were down to the lead-line event, where the dismounted rider, facing the horse but away from it on a long rein so as to give the judges an unhindered view, must make the horse "stand." Sally Rawlings was leading Platonica, followed by Julie with Snappy.

They circled, turned, and stopped.

Platonica's wonky knee locked. She swayed, came upright, and froze. In swaying, she had brushed the big man's thoroughbred just as he moved it into position.

The glossy stallion took Platonica's touch to be, if not shameless invitation, then definitely a show of interest, and though he remained in place, his response was sufficient to cause an awed Willie Whittle to shout, "Look at that!" The judges did, and that was the end of the thoroughbred.

Willie's sudden cry had made Platonica's ears shoot up straight, which, with her knee causing her to lock in an absolutely square position, was just what the judges were looking for. Sally and Platonica placed first.

Heather Spooner reminded the younger kids on the way home that the success was the result of hard work and proper training. And, she thought to herself, not a small amount of good old horse sense.

Mr. Mayhem

Elliott Smalley's eyes sparkled behind his bi-focals. "I'm talking *characters!*" he hooted and slapped his knee.

They were in the Legion, Elliott almost wriggling as he waited for the ferry bringing one of his old newspapering pals for an afternoon's visit.

"Joe Milligan! Listen—they sent us out, me and him, to cover the Doukhobors when they marched from the Kootenays clear down to Victoria Square and ended up taking their clothes off and setting fire to them. We were broke and Joe was thirsty. He takes off 'round the corner and comes back with a hubcap from some giant Buick.

" 'Help the Doukhobor kiddies,' he shouts, passing it like a collection plate. 'Help the little children.' He got nine bucks in quick time and we spent the rest of the day drinking beer in the Lotus Hotel. He filed the story from the bar phone while I stood at the window giving him a crowd count.

"He said he preferred to use his own quotes because the kind of people that would be attracted to that kind of event might be capable of saying just about anything! 'You can't trust them to get it right, Elliott.' he told me! And now he's publisher of one of the biggest papers in the east. *Publisher*, for god's sake!"

Elliott slapped the table, and half of his drink slopped from the glass. "I'm telling you—we were wild!"

Samson Spinner measured the comfortably filled tweed suit, the bifocals, and the artfully combed surviving hair. He glanced at the glass of white wine spritzer, and considered the probability of a wild Elliott Smalley. He grinned as a line from somewhere tickled his mind, something about ". . . that old, bald cheater, Time . . ."

The *Gulf Queen* blasted three times and Elliott jumped to his feet.

"Just hang around a while," he said, with a knowing grin.

"And this is Joe Milligan!" Elliott announced half an hour later, "the original Mr. Mayhem! Set 'em up!" he called to the bar steward.

"Ah, Perrier, please, Elliott," the visitor said.

Elliott laughed. "Rye with a chaser—right?"

"Perrier," said the visitor. He glanced around the Legion lounge, and sniffed. "If they stock it," he added.

He brushed a piece of invisible lint from his impeccable navy blazer as Elliott made introductions, then stroked the knife-edged crease in his grey slacks. Samson's eyes widened momentarily as Elliott set down a glass of draft and a shot of rye for himself, and the pale Perrier for his guest.

"So you're Joe Milligan," Samson laughed. "Well, we certainly know all about you!"

The visitor looked at him for some seconds. "At the very best that's an extravagant claim, Mr. Spinner," he said. "Your facts would have to be suspect." He smiled—a thin little motion. "As you must know from Elliott, we are respecters of nothing if not facts in the world of journalism."

Samson glanced at Elliott, who blushed. The visitor gave a satisfied nod and accepted the glass of mineral water from Elliott. Elliott sipped his draft and touched his lips to the whisky. Samson suppressed a chuckle as Elliott shuddered.

"I was telling them about the Doukhobor story," Elliott chuckled. "Your 'collection plate,' remember?"

A frown ridged the visitor's brow.

Elliott stood. "Help the little Doukhobor kiddies," he chanted, holding out an imaginary hubcap, and sat down howling and wiping his eyes.

Milligan shook his head. "You've got me there, Elliott," he said.

Elliott stared at him, then laughed. The sound was a little ragged.

"Hey," he said, "remember those two girls at the Hotel Vancouver, the two you thought were with the church convention and they turned out to be. . . . "

Milligan was shaking his head. "No I don't," he said. "I don't think I was there for any of that, Elliott. I do know there were some pretty grubby characters in the newsroom in those days," he said. "You're probably thinking of one of them. They wouldn't get away with any of that in my newsroom," he said. "I run a tight ship."

He started looking at his watch. "Let's go see this paper of yours," he said.

Elliott made a pass at the draft, ignored the rye, and they left.

Later, as he sat with a fresh spritzer before him, he shook his head and frowned.

"It all happened just as I said, you know," he told Samson. He looked down at his suit and flicked off a piece of lint. "You'd wonder," he said, "how a person could change so much. Wouldn't you?"

Scratch and Sin

The Reverend Randall Rawlings waved the shiny scratch-and-win lottery ticket. The face on it—that of a bearded pioneer—looked down on the congregation in the little Church in the Vale.

"Even in the collection plate!" the vicar railed. "Nobody minds a little flutter, but this business is getting out of hand!"

He crumpled the offending ducat and dropped it to the pulpit floor, at the same time deliberately wiping his fingers on his surplice. The Reverend Rawlings had picked gambling as the sin of the week.

What set him off, he said, were the long lineups that had sprouted at Charlie Logan's store since Charlie became an agent for the lotteries. Wish-waiters, he called them, with some disdain.

He refrained from mentioning that the take at the church bingo had dropped measurably since Charlie started selling tickets and that the chance of getting the rest of the money for the new mini-bus for the old folks at Pioneer Hall was looking thin indeed.

He finished up by telling them they'd likely find better odds in a good old-fashioned prayer, and led them in lowering heads. As he thought on the good things, the vicar's half-closed eyes caught the reflected twinkle in those of the pioneer on the bent ticket on the floor. He scrunched his eyes shut and finished the prayer.

Miss Bell-Atkinson congratulated him on the sermon as the congregation filed out. "It's a rare kind of courage that will confront that kind of creeping vice these days, Vicar," she declared.

The Reverend Rawlings inclined his head modestly. The bingo figures flickered past his eyes, and he blushed slightly. He caught the eye of one of Miss Bell-Atkinson's twin nephews, Henry and/or Harvey, as the pair passed, and noted the little snicker. Either one of them was capable of slipping the ticket into the collection plate.

He picked the ticket from the pulpit floor as he headed for the house and some lunch, and dropped it into the wastepaper basket in his study. Then he retrieved it and flattened it out on his desk. The pioneer was Joe Whitehead, "the man who brought the iron horse west." A good likeness, too, the vicar thought, as he studied the blunt, rather dour features.

He sat down at the desk and studied the ticket, and shook his head. Then he erased one of the six tiny embossed shields on the grey foil box in the top right corner and exposed "$2." He threw the ticket back in the waste basket, stood, sat down, frowned, and picked it out again. He erased another shield and exposed "$10,000." "Hrrrmph," he said, erased another, and uncovered "$5." He crumpled the ticket up. Then he straightened it again and erased a fourth shield and disclosed another "$2."

"Suckers!" he said. Angrily he rubbed away another shield and exposed "$10,000." The vicar's breath sucked in like that of a man recently shot. He stared at the small shield covering the sixth and final figure.

The face of Joe Whitehead stared up at him, by now somewhat crinkled from the various foldings and reparations. A sudden shaft of sunlight landed on him and the old railroader seemed to wink. The vicar took the pencil eraser and tentatively touched the opaque foil. He rubbed gently on one corner, and saw a zero. A small fist grabbed the Reverend Randall Rawlings somewhere in his middle and squeezed. He rubbed again.

It was some time later that the Reverend Rawlings sat staring at the wall in his study. A picture of Henry and/or Harvey, snickering, flashed past, and the vicar barely suppressed a most un-Christian guffaw. He started riffling through the yellow pages, looking for automobile dealers in Victoria. He stopped for a moment and looked up toward the ceiling.

"Thank you," he said and chuckled.

Lucy Holds the Fort

The arrival of RCMP Constable Lucy Strutter to fill in for a couple of weeks for Constable Jean LaFleur did not sit well with the Brigadier.

"Women make excellent mothers and nurses," he said. "And some of them were dashed good ambulance drivers in the war—once you taught them to sort out the gears. Not cut out for police work, though. Not for a minute. Too soft, don't you see?"

And he very soon started finding evidence to support his position. Lucy stopped two of the Brannigan kids in possession of a suspiciously large number of chocolate bars and moving at a fast clip away from Charlie Logan's store.

"Juvenile court!" sputtered the Brigadier. "That's where the little buggers should have gone. Cut their hair and lock them away for a bit. Bread and water. Shape 'em up! Know what she did? Drove them back to Logan's, got them to apologise—then bought them each one of the damned things they had purloined!"

She had pulled over young Edward Plummer who, in Chief Jimmy's Oldsmobile, had made the Brigadier's remaining hair stand on end when he passed the old soldier's Mini-minor on the narrowest part of Ennerdale Road at a high rate of speed.

"Wagged her finger at him and told him not to do it again!" the Brigadier said disgustedly.

And then she had stood by and actually smiled when Singlestar, the more-or-less leader of the 1960s leftovers, picketed the front door of the Legion for a couple of hours, protesting the continuing military presence ensconced there.

So it was with a distinctly sinking feeling that the Brigadier watched the trio of punks come off the *Gulf Queen* flourishing their hunting rifles and several cases of beer. The Brigadier felt duty bound to stop them and advise that shotguns and slugs only are allowed for deer. He also pointed out that booze and firearms are a very poor combination. At which point, the biggest of the three, a lank-haired lout of considerable size, told the Brigadier very precisely what to do with his advice. Then he went a step further, prodding the older man to punctuate his points, while his two partners punched each other on the shoulder and fell about laughing.

Lucy pulled up in the squad car about then, and asked them what they thought they were doing. The big one sized her up—the cute nose and fresh complexion and the even, white smile which hadn't quite reached her eyes on this occasion—and he went back to tormenting the Brigadier.

Lucy sighed and climbed out of the car. The Brigadier was about to tell her to get back in the vehicle when Lucy tapped the big fellow with her flashlight. It looked like nothing, and the Brigadier was amazed at how the young man's nasty laughter changed into a kind of whimper as he grabbed his wrist.

One of his friends took two steps towards Lucy and she turned and there was the flashlight again and the second fellow was clutching himself sort of low and centre and letting out little retching sounds. Lucy turned to the third one, who stepped back quickly, his hands cupped low, and she said, "Now you be real good boys, OK?"

He was slow in replying and Lucy stepped forward, and he said, "Yes ma'am!" right sharply. The trio went back on the first ferry the next morning, without any meat.

Lucy was catching the night ferry, the one that brought Jean LaFleur back, and there was a nice-sized group to see her off. The Brigadier stepped out of the pack and harrumphed a bit. "There were some," he said, searching the audience for the perpetrators and nodding accusingly, "who actually questioned your ability to handle the job."

He took her hand. "Let me tell them," he said, "and let me tell you—Constable Lucy Strutter—you're a damned good man!"

With a Little Help

The Brannigan family's first Christmas in the Inlet was shaping up as a bleak one. And Anwen Brannigan's streak of stubborn, Celtic independence was not helping.

"We don't need charity hampers, thank you," she had advised Samson Spinner when he knocked on the door of the place she and her seven youngsters had moved into in the summer. There has been no sign of a Mr. Brannigan, and apart from a little hell-raising by the four boys, the family has kept to itself.

Samson was prepared to argue, but the look in the early-old, deep-blue eyes warned against it, and he stepped back as she shut the door. He returned with the case of assorted goods to the community hall and slammed it down on a bench.

The Brigadier shrugged. "Well, you can't force them to take it, can you?"

Samson nodded, agreed that indeed you can't, and left. That was a week before Christmas Eve.

The next day Anwen Brannigan was passing Logan's store when

Charlie rushed out and stopped her. His wife had been felled by the flu, he explained, and he desperately needed a hand for a couple of days on the till. He would pay seven dollars an hour, and at Christmas, the staff got a 75% discount on everything. And, he fretted, there were two turkeys left in the freezer that obviously nobody was going to buy, and the freezer had to be cleaned and serviced . . . she would be doing him a favour. . . . Half an hour later Anwen was ringing up groceries.

At about the same time, the Brannigan youngsters were running into some good fortune. Timmy, the youngest, had his name pulled out of the hat at school as winner of the raffle for the brand-new BMX bike with knobby tires. When he said he didn't think he had even bought a ticket, young Julie Martin said, "You must have, you dummy, you won it," and Timmy fell before her gap-filled grin and logic.

Two of the three Brannigan girls, Morag and Megan, found themselves part of a spontaneous lunchtime song festival at the community hall and were judged the winners by Miss Bell-Atkinson. The mystery prizes, to be delivered, wrapped, the next night, were an acoustic guitar for Morag, who could pick a tune on a pitchfork, and a parcel of L.M. Montgomery books for Megan, who has been known to announce that she is the spirit of Anne Shirley of Green Gables.

The other four young Brannigans turned out to be Godsends during an unprecedented epidemic of emergency-employment situations. Heather Spooner collared Rory and Mick to do an urgent cleanup of her stables at the riding school, paying them double time after 4:30 PM. She was also able to talk them into coming down once a day over the imminent two-week school break to exercise any horse they figured looked in need, for half an hour at a time. Rory said he might have to come twice a day to do a decent job.

Brenda, the oldest Brannigan, and her brother Finbar spent a whole day looking after Rachel Spinner's kennels and brushing the silken coats of five setter bitches and a tumble of velvet puppies after Rachel was called away at short notice. Rachel later said they were true guardians of the gates and stuffed almost as much money into each of their pockets as their mother was being paid at Logan's store.

All the kids were waiting outside the last night when Anwen said goodnight to Charlie Logan and left the store. They fell in together as they started home up Ennerdale Road, with Timmy's oafish dog O'Toole bringing up the rear. One of them started singing, and the others joined in, harmonizing. "Oh, Little Town of Bethlehem. . . . "

They finished that and kept on walking, and a small, clear voice started "Away in a Manger. . . . "

Samson Spinner came over the crest of the hill and slowed the van as he drew alongside the Brannigans. "Merry Christmas, Brannigans!" he called out. There was a momentary silence, then Anwen Brannigan laughed. Her head came up and her blue eyes glittered. "Yes," she called. "Merry Christmas!"

As Samson drove slowly away he could hear the young Brannigans joining in, like bells on the night air: "Merry Christmas! Merry Christmas! Merry Christmas. . . "

One Day a Child Was Born

There's one youngster in Spinner's Inlet who'll be having a houseful of visitors on Christmas Day. His dad, José, said he would kill a goat for the occasion. Miss Bell-Atkinson said she'd have no part of eating anyone's goat, and that they certainly do have strange practices, these Mexicans, don't they? But she'll surely be there because . . . well, we have to go back to the summer the Estradas arrived.

They got off the ferry, José Estrada Moreno and his young wife, in a pickup truck that had observers holding their breath as it groaned up the slope from the dock. It turned out they had got landed-immigrant status after three years of trying, and with help from a cousin in Kamloops who had then disappeared. Somebody had told them there was plenty of cheap housing on the island and they had believed it.

They arrived on the Saturday of Labour Day weekend, always the busiest of the year. The Cedars Lodge was packed with divers from the Okanagan. And down at the government campsite, budding Baden-Powells were bunking in the trees. They spent the first night in the truck. They were like fawns and had about nine words of English between them.

They ended up making a deal with Charlie Logan for the small barn on the west side of Keswick Creek. You should see that old barn now. The tools José had in the back of the pickup certainly weren't for show, and he's made a fine, partitioned little house out of the place. As well as that, he hasn't been without a day's work since that first week.

They were terribly shy at the start, keeping to themselves, he building porches and decks and fences with his quiet skill and a soft smile, while she got a vegetable garden going and started up a small herd of goats and chickens.

Maggie Wilson, whose maiden name had been Margarita Consuela Pereyra-Mendez, started visiting and was the first to report that Maria was pregnant. Maggie said the couple was basically shy and that people should leave them alone and they would open up in their own good time.

She did persuade Maria to see Dr. Timothy, who is no stranger to payment in chickens from those without medical coverage. This time he got a split-rail fence of windfall cedar, as neat as a picture, down the side and around the front of the house. Dr. Timothy finally had to get Maggie to tell José to quit and to convince him that he had more than paid for Maria's care throughout the pregnancy. Then Maria went for an early start.

Samson Spinner got the first inkling, late in the evening. There had been reports for a couple of days of a rare cougar-sighting. Young Julie Martin had even claimed in a school essay that she herself had "seen the creetyer's foot prince." Samson heard the sheep muttering and moving about close to the house, and he stepped out to check. It was black dark, blowing, and the rain coming down like nails. Samson chatted with the ewes for a while and was turning to go inside when he saw the light flashing in the distance, from across the creek. It flicked on and off, in a definite pattern.

Then above the driving rain and the wind, Samson heard rushing water. He hunched his shoulders and headed towards the sound. He stopped sharply at the edge of Keswick Creek, which was over its banks and running faster than he could ever recall. The old earth dike, that for years had held back the runoff water in the great alder swamp, had surrendered.

Samson stood on the creek bank and peered across, up the slope to Logan's barn, where the lantern continued flashing. And now he heard, faintly, José's voice, "Maria. . . baby. . . Maria. . . baby. . . " and each word was whipped away by the wind.

"Oh, God," Samson said, and stepped back as a rush of new water filled his shoes. The creek was spreading into a small lake that isolated the barn. A man would be able to wade through it, certainly not a vehicle.

Samson yelled into the wind: "José! OK! Pronto! Momento! Hang on buddy—I hear you! Mucho bueno!" His Spanish all used up, he turned and ran. He knew the Estradas had no phone. Neither, it turned out, did Dr. Timothy right then; the lines were down again.

Samson jumped into the van and hurled it down the driveway, scattering bleating sheep and shouting ducks. He skidded out onto Asby Road, where he avoided an unhappy event only because of the blaring horn and flashing headlights of the Wilson truck driven by young Charlie, who since acquiring his licence has been virtually living in the vehicle.

Samson put Charlie to work. "Stay by the creek till we get back.

Shout at him—tell him the doctor's on his way. If you have to, swear in Spanish, like your mother does."

Dr. Timothy abandoned his chessboard and half a pint of mulled wine, and a short time later he, Samson, and Charlie stepped into the frigid water which slapped them at mid-thigh and threatened to knock them off their feet. Samson gasped something about brass monkeys and Charlie snickered, then went back to hollering at José, who was still waving the lantern at the heavens which continued to pour down on all of them.

José went down on his knees when they came out of the water, dripping and shivering, and started rattling on too fast for even Charlie, but Dr. Timothy just headed for the barn, water and weeds spurting from his wellingtons as he ran.

Maria was in her little bedroom in the corner where the hayracks used to be, and after a quick examination Dr. Timothy told Charlie to tell José to get the kettle going and find clean towels and face cloths and whatever else was around. Maggie said later she wasn't surprised at all how well Charlie came through—that he had always been a bright lad like most of the men on his mother's side.

Samson acted as nurse, and he was the one who finally took the newborn boy and dressed him in a cute little outfit that Maria had made and wrapped him in a blanket and handed him to Maria. She lay back with a look of pure wonder on her face, then smiled at the lot of them as they stood in the doorway.

"Let her sleep now," Dr. Timothy said, and the three of them and José stepped out.

The storm was quieting, and José's young Belgian mare and the goats were snuffling outside, where the ragged clouds sailed across the moon and some clearing spots showed stars in clusters.

Samson laughed softly and shook his head. "Fantastic," he said. Then he asked José if they had picked a name for the kid.

José didn't answer, so Samson went into body language and slow, loud syllables to start repeating the question. José smiled and held up a hand. "Iss okay, Samson, I honnerstan."

Then José looked at the small clock on the wall, which showed 2:30 AM on Christmas Day. He glanced out the window and up to the stars, and named his baby, and the three of them told him that was most certainly a wonderful idea. Samson, Dr. Timothy and young Charlie will be very special guests at the celebration to honour the first anniversary of the birth of the baby Jesus Estrada Moreno.

Blowin' in the Wind

Constable Jean LaFleur flinched and looked up as a ferocious gust from the southeaster outside clattered a hemlock branch against the roof of the detachment's rented cottage. He was going through a sheaf of Ottawa's daily crime bulletins—details of those wanted and suspected—which arrive in Spinner's Inlet at the whim of Canada Post. He started reading a list of names and descriptions, and froze at the third one down.

"Louis Rioux, 19." He read the rest: "Suspected thief and con man. Says he's seeking work, ingratiates himself, leaves with money and valuables. No convictions. Two suspected offences in Quebec and Alberta."

Jean had picked the young man up shortly after he trudged off the ferry carrying his backpack. He'd said he was looking for work, and that he'd been on the road for two years, working here and there, after leaving a hopeless family situation in Quebec City. They had traded opinions about the Canadiens and the Expos and had agreed that playing for either one likely would be better than working for a living.

The young Mountie cursed and looked out the window as another massive gust shook the house and set a line of alders dancing. He had liked the youngster and had taken him right then to the Spinner home, where Samson was starting work on a new boathouse for the water taxi and was looking, he said, for reliable help.

Samson weighed the young Quebecer up, and started him at $8.50 an hour plus accommodation in one of the several self-contained cabins around the place. That was two weeks ago, and Samson said the kid was doing fine. He was paying him $10.50 now, and every nickel earned.

"And 'e is learn the Hinglish real good," Samson had joked.

Real funny, Jean LaFleur thought. He picked up his hat and set it squarely on his head, and picked up the bulletin. He stepped outside, ducking against the wild blasts coming off the water, climbed into the patrol car, and headed for the Spinner property.

Samson read the bulletin, and grunted. "He told me he owes some money to some people and is working to pay them back," he said. "He seemed a little bit sheepish." He tapped the paper. "But I don't think he knows he's on one of these."

"Where is he?" the Mountie said.

Talk about sheepish looks.

"He, ah, he went into Vancouver this morning," Samson said. "I gave him a cheque, signed, for him to make out to whichever lumber yard he chose to order the shipment from. I told him he could go up to $1,800."

Jean LaFleur's eyes did a genuine Gallic flip.

When the *Gulf Queen* came sliding in toward the dock in the evening, Jean LaFleur and Samson were sitting together in the squad car. The wind was as bad as ever, coming in huge, uneven blasts, rocking the police vehicle.

A dozen foot passengers were waiting to walk off the car deck, staggering with the swells as the ferry elbowed its way into the berth. Samson could make out the tall shape of the vicar at the front, and the substantial one of Miss Bell-Atkinson beside him. Two of the

Plummer boys were there, striding off together, and turning and laughing at something that Louis Rioux said as he followed them.

Samson turned to Jean LaFleur, a smile starting in his eyes. Jean LaFleur's face was tight. The Plummer boys and the young Quebecer approached the car, and Jean LaFleur climbed out, facing them. The young man stopped as he saw the constable's eyes on him, and the expression, and his laughter, faded. He glanced from Jean LaFleur's face to the paper in his hand.

The constable winced as the wind gathered for another blow, and he grabbed his hat. As he did, the wind grasped the paper, and took it. Jean LaFleur grabbed for it, and missed. Louis Rioux snatched at it too, and then tried to trap it with his foot as it swooped and flew past him.

Another mad gust took the paper and hurled it over the dock railing and out onto the rolling waters of Spinner's Inlet, where it floated for a moment, then disappeared under the bubbles and foam.

Samson was out of the car, and he waited while Jean LaFleur accepted the loss of the paper then brought his eyes back to Rioux. The wind had settled for the moment, and the policeman adjusted his hat.

The young man spoke first. "Was that somet'ing important?" he asked.

Constable Jean LaFleur considered the question. He turned toward the car as they felt another blast building. "I'm not sure," he said.

He climbed into the car. Rioux waited. Jean LaFleur examined him. "But I don't think so," he added.

Tub or Not Tub

The deputy minister had come to explain to the seniors at Pioneer Hall why their request for a grant couldn't be approved. "Hot tubs," he said, his fingers making a tent, "don't come under the heading of either recreation or health items. They are more of a luxury object, and right now the budget stops short of luxuries."

Samantha Pringle, who is 79, told the deputy minister that last year on a weekend outing to Vancouver she and Henry Arrowsmith, who is 81, had been invited to a home with a hot tub and told to enjoy it, and if he didn't think that they had had some grand recreation, she had some particular news for him.

Henry said damrights it was recreational because he had also earlier hot-tubbed it in Victoria with Harriet Mosely, who is 75, and that it had been about as recreational as you could get, to say nothing about healthful and generally beneficial.

"It's something in the water that does it, I believe," Henry said.

Samantha said she didn't know that Henry had done it earlier with Harriet—"tubbing, that is"—but that the information did explain several things she had wondered about since she and Henry did it. "Tubbing, that is," she said. She told Henry there was something she wanted to discuss with him when the meeting was over.

The bulk of the money for the proposed hot-tub area had already been raised, by the Legion and the Spinner's Inlet Seniors Welfare Committee. All that was needed, committee chairman Samson Spinner told the man from Victoria, was about $10,000 for the actual tubs and the jet motors. All the plumbing and wiring work was already volunteered.

The civil servant, a bit of a prim fellow in his early 60s, with long side-hair combed vainly back across a clearly barren scalp, shook his head and flicked through several more pages of his manual on grants for recreation. He asked if they had considered perhaps something like large-sized chess or checkers tables, designed for easier movement by older people?

Robinson Sparks, who is 88, adjusted his hearing aid, said there was no one he knew who had trouble with his movements, and if there was, by God, a game of chess was not the solution. What was needed, he said, and which would keep everybody loose, sort of, was hot tubs, goddammit, and that was what they wanted. Robinson's voice was rising and he started thrashing an empty chair with his cane as he argued. He asked the deputy minister what the government hypocrites who waste half their time spending taxpayers' money in California have against hot tubs, and when the man found a page and started reading from it, Robinson shouted at him to shut up if that's the best he could do.

Agnes Merriweather, buxom at 66, who had enjoyed five husbands in a 50-year career in the fashion business, asked the deputy minister if he had ever been in a hot tub with a really good friend, and if he hadn't, would he like to try the experience before he left so as to have a better idea of what it was all about?

She said that while they didn't have a hot tub exactly, yet, if he would like to step across to her apartment they could simulate the experience in her bathtub. She said she and Henry Arrowsmith had tried it out a couple of times, and with the bathtub full to the brim you could hardly tell the difference.

Harriet Mosely quickly added that she and Henry had tried the same test several times in her bathtub, *and* in Henry's bathtub, and found it to be fairly satisfactory, although Henry had had to frequently leap quickly to his feet because one of his knees kept locking, but that wouldn't happen in a real hot tub where there was more room to manoeuvre.

Samantha Pringle said rather stiffly that it was clear that Henry had been performing far above and beyond the call of duty, but that if anyone should know about the benefits of hot tubs, Henry certainly should.

The deputy minister declined Agnes's invitation to test the waters, saying he really didn't have time, but he said he was impressed with the degree of research that had been done, especially by Henry Arrowsmith, and he appeared to be on the verge of smiling.

Samson Spinner drove the deputy minister back down for the Victoria ferry. The deputy minister said he had heard that Gulf Islands people had a particular zest for life, and that was clearly so.

"I think," the man said, "there are times when the department has to be flexible, wouldn't you say?" and Samson said he would indeed. The man said he would commend the health arguments made to him at Pioneer Hall, and that they could expect to hear from him soon.

Then he remarked that, as a widower who liked to get about a good bit, he had been planning to spend some time in the general area of Spinner's Inlet and just out of curiosity, did Samson know if Mrs. Merriweather was usually around on weekends?

Water Ways

Some of the wells at the south end were already low again, which had people recalling last summer's drought. "Don't rush to flush," was a common sign posted on bathroom doors for the benefit of mainland visitors who never have to face the problem, other than being told when they can water their lawns.

Lennie Wilson was much more colourful, but his rhyming admonition to guests about how many times they could do which before they flushed—although admired in certain quarters and recited often in the Legion—was flatly rejected by the Chamber of Commerce for its Save-the-Water poster campaign.

"The man's a boor," said Miss Bell-Atkinson.

The Martin girls got into trouble over a tree frog they adopted and named Bandit. They kept sneaking pans of water down behind the big weeping willow for his ablutions. When their mother caught them, the little one, Julie, waggled a finger: "He'll dry up and his eyes will drop off and his bones will stick out everywhere," she said.

Sheila Martin decided she couldn't have that on her conscience and told her husband Paul that he was probably right after all and that, yes, the two of them would have to start taking more showers together to conserve water. Paul told the girls that saving frogs was a major act of compassion that likely would bring them a Greenpeace award, and that they should start looking for more of the little buggers.

The Slaters were in great shape. Ever since they drilled their well and inadvertently tapped the supply that Froelich had considered his own, they've had loads and Froelich's had his tongue hanging out. They let him, to the amazement of many, fill his swimming pool after he pleaded the pending visit of rich and very old relatives from the prairies—and then when the Slater kids put on their swimsuits and went and hung around the gate to the pool and smiled at him, he told them to bugger off and to learn some respect for private property.

Charlie Logan at the store had anticipated the drought. Inspired by TV ads for "bottled pure natural water" that they sell in California, he acquired a 30,000-gallon tank that filled nicely in early spring. Charlie apparently didn't get the whole recipe for pure. His first customers were campers from Vancouver, and when Charlie opened the tap to fill their jugs they watched wide-eyed at the things that came out, and said that if they had known about this, they would have brought their fishing gear.

Charlie said that only softies from the city would be bothered by a few polliwogs and that at least it showed the water was life-sustaining, didn't it?

Rachel Spinner built a dam across Keswick Creek so that her Derwent Kennel guests would not go short of bath and shampoo. This was considered poor sport by the Swede, who has a complex irrigation system downstream to support his vegetable garden. He tried to reason with Rachel, but she wouldn't listen, so Svensen acquired a couple of sticks of powder and blew the dam halfway to Victoria. Two of Rachel's setter bitches gave birth prematurely, and a high-strung Afghan that she had been boarding for some posh people on Saltspring cleared the fence and skulked howling in the bush for three weeks afterwards.

Chief Jimmy Plummer said thing were getting out of hand and he organized a rain dance, which he said he had learned while visiting some cousins in Alberta. He decked himself out in feathers, leggings and moccasins and put on such an astonishing performance down at the ferry dock that a gaggle of American tourists started throwing money. Two weeks later, it was hotter and drier than ever and Chief Jimmy wondered aloud if maybe he had screwed things up and done the sun dance instead. He said he would check with his cousins the next time he went to Alberta.

They're saying it's going to be another long, hot one this year. Sheila Martin has been heard reminding the girls to keep an eye out for tree frogs in trouble.

Psychic Sidekicks

"Don't laugh, Samson," Barbara Spinner said. "It's in the blood. You could have a touch yourself. It pops up all the time."

Samson Spinner snorted. "You won't be satisfied until you have a resident witch," he said.

He left his mother setting out places for a Saturday-morning meeting of the Spinner's Inlet Psychic Society. He got back at noon, just as young Julie and Jillian Martin landed for a visit. The kids are family, through their great-grandmother, Victoria Spinner.

"You should have been here earlier, girls," Samson said. "You could have got right into the spirit of things."

Jillian gave him a little smile. Barbara sniffed and left for the market. Jillian settled down at the kitchen table with a book of crossword puzzles, while her sister took off outside with Samson's border collie, Patch. Samson poured a coffee and started reading the paper.

He turned a page and Jillian, her head down and scribbling vigorously, muttered, "You want me to get that, Samson?"

Samson looked up. "What?" he said.

She looked at Samson, a little frown starting. Then she turned toward the telephone on the kitchen counter. Samson started to speak again, and the phone rang. A smile replaced the youngster's frown.

"I'll get it," said Samson, and he shot her a quizzical look as he crossed the room. It was Thelma Spooner reminding him they had an arrangement for dinner that night at her place.

Samson quietly asked Thelma if she knew anything about mind-reading. Thelma said she could read his mind any time but it was not the kind of thing she liked to talk about on the phone, what with party lines being all ears. Maybe later, she said, and giggled. Samson went back to the paper.

"You sweet on Thelma Spooner, Samson?" Jillian said, with a grin.

"Who said anything about Thelma?" he said.

Jillian shrugged. "Just asking," she said.

They were quiet for a while, then she started humming "Where Have All the Flowers Gone," and Samson delighted her by joining in and singing it right through.

He switched on the radio for the news, and the lamenting voices of Mary Travers and Peter and Paul were just posing the question, "Oh, when will they ever learn? When will they ever learn?" Jillian was smiling and swaying with the beat.

Samson stared at her. "All right," he said. "What's next?"

She looked up. "Next what?"

"On the radio. The next song."

She looked at him as if he had grown another head. "How should I know?" she said, and added, "Sheeeesh," and went back to her puzzles.

Samson returned to his reading. Then he said, "How about some lunch?"

She nodded, and Samson headed for the kitchen. He was reaching into the cupboard when she called, "We already had macaroni and cheese twice this week, Samson."

Samson stared at her, but her head was down again and her pencil busy. "Pancakes, then," said Samson, changing cupboards. She joined him in the kitchen.

"I'll empty the dishwasher, Samson, or there won't be enough plates and stuff."

Samson put the pancake mix down. "Who said it's all in the dishwasher?"

She shrugged. "Well, it always is when you want it, isn't it?"

She had a point, Samson thought. But he watched her as she reached unerringly in and brought out the four blue plates with the cornflower borders that he had known he would use.

Barbara Spinner came in just then. She hugged Jillian and asked her where her sister was.

"I don't know," said Jillian, and Samson snorted loud enough for his mother to turn around and examine him. He started plopping batter on the griddle. Barbara went to call the younger one, who came tumbling through the back door, whooping and laughing with the dog tangled up in her legs.

They started on the pancakes, and Samson debated whether to raise the question with his mother. But that would make him as daft as the rest of them, he thought. Forget it. He was letting the spook brigade get to him. He said nothing, and Barbara left the room.

Samson looked over at the two girls, blonde hair hanging over the plates as they laid into the pancakes and gulped their milk and he laughed at himself.

"Hey, you guys," he said, "I got an idea."

Young Julie looked up at her sister and they locked eyes for a second. Then the little one turned to Samson.

"Thank you, Samson," she said. "But we really don't want to go fishing today."

Smokin' 'em Out

Sebastian Whittle's crusade to stamp out smoking around Spinner's Inlet has been less than a flaming success. Sebastian, who had his first puff about 40 years ago when he was six, quit cold turkey several months ago and, in the relentless spirit of the born-again, has been an avenging force for healthy pink lungs ever since.

He even has a sign on the outside of his ticket booth at the ferry, advising all those getting on or off the *Gulf Queen* that they are leaving or entering "a smoke-free zone."

"This is a worldwide movement, you know," he advised the Brigadier, at a thorny meeting of the golf club executive where Sebastian had hidden all the ashtrays and Wilson Spinner as president refused to call things to order until they were replaced.

"So is Communism," said the Brigadier, puffing aggressively on one of his pungent Gauloises, which he says are the only good things to come out of France since the Allies left.

Sebastian has alienated many—including Miss Bell-Atkinson, who usually is right at the head of any new move aimed at the improvement of other people. However, she occasionally affects one of those pastel Russian cigarettes that she sticks in the kind of long holder that was fashionable up to about the 1940s. With her eyes half-shut she likes to think it gives her a certain mystique. Most people just figure she's squinting to keep the smoke out of her eyes.

She was trailing a wisp of smoke the other day when she went into Logan's store and asked Charlie to cut her some nice rashers of bacon. Sebastian quietly moved down an aisle until he was close enough to her smoke to reasonably be offended, and started on at her.

"You realize you are fouling the air that I have to breathe, don't you?" he said.

Miss Bell-Atkinson inhaled deeply, leaned over, and sent a stream of second-hand smoke straight toward Sebastian's nose. She then very succinctly stated what her preference would be on the two options that Sebastian has concerning breathing.

Sebastian then advanced on Charlie Logan and lectured him on his obligations to the health of the shopping public. "You should have a sign up," Sebastian said.

"You're right," said Charlie, and he came out from behind the counter with a blue-felt-pen "Special of the Week" card that he stuck on a stack of cartons of Players Light.

"How's that?" he said.

Sebastian has been after Dr. Timothy, of course, and finally got him to sign his petition, which he plans to send to tobacco companies asking them to go out of business for the good of the community. Dr. Timothy mumbled something about also getting in touch with the Tooth Fairy, while he signed it.

Sebastian later took the petition to the golf club and found Dr. Timothy behind an acrid blue cloud rising out of the pipeful of black shag that he likes to have with a pint of dark draft when he finishes the back nine. Sebastian delivered a quite biting harangue about Hippocrates and hypocrisy until Dr. Timothy told him to shut up and bugger off. Dr. Timothy said the trouble with fanatics is that they take everything to extremes.

Sebastian tried his luck down at the fish dock, where Chief Jimmy Plummer was sucking on the muddy end of a crumbling half-stogie while deftly skinning and filleting a surprised-looking rock cod. Chief Jimmy advised Sebastian before he could get rolling that his family over the centuries has smoked many things, including a lot of fish and, when the cause was just, several white men, so if Sebastian wouldn't mind. . . .

Sebastian went to the Legion where he declared he was sick of trying to save people from themselves and they could smoke until they dropped dead. Then he pulled a newspaper clipping out of his pocket and asked if anyone there realized that more than a couple of ounces of booze a day could mean death to their liver?

The Vicar's Ferry Tale

The Reverend Randall Rawlings winced when he saw the lineup for the night ferry to Victoria. He had left it late, and it was clearly going to be a toss-up whether there'd be room on the *Gulf Queen* for all the cars. He had to be on the ferry. Young Sally was returning from a week's youth camp at Friday Harbor and he'd arranged to meet her at Sidney.

The vicar would have made it, if the young man in the flashy maroon pickup hadn't jumped the line. He muscled around the Reverend's veteran Volvo and was onto the ramp and into the last available space on the *Queen* before Rawlings knew it. The fellow wasn't about to back off, either.

"You were too slow, Bishop," he said. "God helps them that helps themselves, eh? Do unto others before they do it to you, right?" and he laughed.

Sebastian Whittle had been too busy collecting fares from late foot passengers to see exactly which vehicle had arrived when, and couldn't take sides. The deck crew were sympathetic to the vicar, but also were anxious to get going.

The vicar examined the grinning young man in the pickup, and nodded. "Let me get my stuff," he said to Sebastian. "I'll catch a ride from Swartz Bay." He lifted a tote bag from the Volvo's back seat, then went and opened the trunk and clattered around inside. He zippered the bag closed and hurried down onto the car deck.

"Very Christian of you, Padre," the young man said. He waved an open beer can, and the metallic-haired girl with him giggled.

Chief Jimmy Plummer was passing, and that took care of the

vicar's ride at the other end. The Plummer twins, John and James, chatted to one of the crew members. The boys examined the young man in the pickup as the ferry backed out. Then they went upstairs and joined Chief Jimmy and the vicar in the coffee line. The couple from the pickup followed, grinning at the vicar as they passed.

The vicar and the Plummers took a table and settled down. They were soon joined by Clement Shaver, a Victoria car dealer with a cottage in the Inlet. Clement has acquired dubious local recognition for his role in the television commercial in which he and a number of colleagues in uniform blazers attempt to persuade the public that the best automobiles are available from the town fool.

As usual, Clement had a deal for the vicar on the Volvo. And as usual the vicar declined, pointing out quite correctly that the Volvo is in better health than most cars half its age, thanks to the skills he acquired in various service stations as a young man paying his way through school.

The Plummer boys rose and announced with elaborate casualness that they were going for a walk around the boat. The announcement came immediately after the fragrant passing-by of two unaccompanied and thinly clad young ladies in their blossoming late teens, and Chief Jimmy rolled his eyes at the vicar. The boys were gone 20 minutes and returned looking quite pleased with themselves.

Soon the vicar rose and excused himself. He bent and picked up his bag. He smiled at the young couple as he passed their table, and the girl laughed as her boyfriend made a crack about turning the other cheek. It was a fine trip through the waters of the darkening gulf, the lights in the waterfront and cliff-side homes on Galiano and Saltspring seeming close and friendly.

As the skipper announced ten minutes to Swartz Bay, people shuffled about, checking for car keys and adjusting book markers. The Reverend Rawlings reappeared in the lounge, went to the washroom and came out drying his hands. He nodded and smiled to the couple from the pickup as he headed for the stairs.

The vicar was stowing his tote bag in the back of Chief Jimmy's car when the couple arrived on the car deck, and he looked up as the young man started swearing. The maroon pickup was jacked up and resting squarely on several of the white wooden wheel chocks that the ferry crews use to prevent cars rolling. There was no immediate sign of the truck's four snazzy mag wheels.

A crewman stopped and examined the truck and scratched his head and said that was the first time he'd seen anything like that and wasn't it quite remarkable what people would do these days? The vicar said it certainly was, and he climbed into the front seat of Chief Jimmy's car while the boys got in the back.

The twins were in an unusually philosophical mood, talking suddenly about the shortcomings of some of today's young people. "So many of them just sit there spinning their wheels, going nowhere," James observed. John nodded sagely. "They do seem to lack a certain drive," he said.

Chief Jimmy half-turned to speak, but saw that the vicar had bowed his head and appeared to be conversing quietly with himself. The chief thought he heard something like, "The first shall be last, and the last shall be first," and what might have been a chuckle.

They rolled off the ferry ramp and out onto the Pat Bay Highway, and the vicar checked his watch and was happy. He'd make the Sidney ferry with time to spare.

Joe Flynn's Trucker

Samson Spinner was approaching the end of the story. " . . . and then the old dump truck just rumbled off along Number Six Road and disappeared into the night."

Young Julie Martin squirmed and gritted her teeth, desperate to hang on until Samson finished. "Is that it?" she said. "Is that the end?"

"Shut up!" Her sister, Jillian, banged her in the ribs. "Of *course* it's not the end, dummy!"

Samson waved a hand for peace. "No, it's not. You see, there was something bothering Joe as he watched the truck disappear."

Jillian hugged herself, anticipating the rest. Little Julie's eyes squeezed shut, and she clamped her lips tight.

"There was something wrong," Samson continued. "Joe . . . "

"Samson, I have to *go*! I'm sorry but I have to *go*!" The young one leaped to her feet and shot off toward the bathroom. "Wait!" she called over her shoulder. "Wait 'til I get back, Samson!"

Jillian, nine, two years older than her sister, groaned. "She *always* does that. Mom says the excitement gets to her. Samson—just whisper it, huh?"

"Uh-uh. Not until she gets back."

That was going to take a little longer than they thought. And by the time Julie did return, and the story was concluded, Maggie Wilson down the road would have had her wish for a rock grotto fulfilled—and then some; the vicar would be a much more upright and happier person; Julie herself would have vowed to abandon her usual technique for flushing the john. And Jillian, against her better judgment, would be tinkering with the embarrassing notion of maybe staying awake again on Christmas Eve.

What caused the delay was Svensen's apparent miscalculation in the amount of powder he needed to blast Maggie's grotto out of the rock face in front of the Wilsons' place. For years, Maggie had wanted a permanent location for a nativity scene. When the Swede had finished, Maggie had enough space to fit not only the baby Jesus and his folks, but also a large honking of donkeys, several flights of angels, a couple of watches of shepherds, a complete fanfare of kings, and at least one conclusion of wise men.

Svensen just picked himself out of the ditch after the dust had settled, brushed himself off, and said they sure don't make rock like they used to.

It was while Svensen was priming his charges that Samson had arrived at the Martins' to drop off Christmas presents. He had listened to Jillian inflicting some minor mental anguish on her sister, taunting Julie about her unwillingness to relinquish the possibility that Santa was more than their dad in his old bathrobe.

"For God's sake, Julie, Santa is just a bunch of different fat guys that sit and sweat outside Sears and those places 'cos there's no other jobs," she'd said. "Or it's like Samson, dropping the presents off."

That's when Samson sat down and said he'd just remembered a story his friend Joe Flynn had told him. Jillian awarded him a suspicious look, but she tucked up on the rug with her sister, and listened.

"Joe is a reporter in Vancouver," Samson said. "In 1977 they had a big strike at the papers. It lasted eight months. Joe had two little girls, like you guys, a mortgage, and all the other stuff. He also had an old blue pickup truck, which he used to start a small garbage- and junk-hauling business, to make some money."

The girls held their noses, and Jillian said, "Yuuch."

Samson nodded. "Yeah, it was. Dirty, hard, and sometimes dangerous. He wasn't terribly good at it and he didn't make much of a living. Around Christmas, it was very bad. The weather was rotten and the work just wasn't coming. Then two days before Christmas he got a call to do a really stinking job. A man wanted his compost box dismantled and the heap taken away. Joe's wife, Sally, told him to forget it and stay home, but the man had offered him $55, and Joe said yes.

"He told me it was the worst work he'd ever done, and that by the time he got the stuff emptied down at the Richmond dump, he had sliced a hand open to the bone on a rusty old tin can, he was soaked to his skin, exhausted, and stinking from the stuff in the compost box, much of which he said was trying to get out by itself as he unloaded it."

Both girls placed their hands over their faces.

"But at least he was done, he had $55 in his jeans, and he was headed home to a good fire, his family, and maybe some hot fruit punch."

"Fruit punch, sure. Hah!" said Jillian.

"Joe said Merry Christmas to the guys operating the dump gate who were waiting to close it up, and he drove out," Samson continued. "The rain was falling like knives, and it was black as a coal mine."

Julie shuddered and shifted closer to her sister.

"He'd gone about half a mile when there was a huge bang, as a front tire blew. The truck started sliding right towards one of those disgusting Richmond ditches, with all the rats and stuff."

Jillian shut her eyes.

"He hung on to the wheel, and he managed to stop it at the last minute, right on the edge of the ditch."

At that point in the story, Samson had stopped, his attention caught by the movements of the Reverend Randall Rawlings, down the hill and across the road. The vicar was awkwardly scaling an aluminum extension ladder up to the eaves to service the vicarage Christmas lights.

"Look at that," Samson said. "That's what he was doing last year when the ladder went, wasn't it?"

It was, and the vicar had been walking unevenly, avoiding bending, and visiting a chiropractor in Victoria ever since.

"Come on, Samson!" It was Julie, her thumb briefly out of her mouth.

"Right. Okay. Now then—the only lights on that stretch of the road were from Joe's truck. No street lights, nothing. He got out and went to change the wheel—and he couldn't. For one thing, the lug nuts were rusted on, and Joe didn't have the muscle to move them. And for another, he was missing part of the jack."

The girls groaned.

"Joe said it was one of the worst moments of his life. He was lying

145

half-frozen on the road, in the dark, sodden and bleeding, his knuckles missing chunks from trying to get the wheel off, two days before Christmas. He said that he was about ready to cry."

"Wow," said the young one.

"And then, suddenly, from along the road behind him,"

"Santa and Rudolph, right?" said Jillian, and howled as her sister belted her and said, "Don't interrupt!"

"No," Samson continued. "It was a dump truck. An old red-and-cream-painted dump truck. It stopped, and the driver climbed down. He looked at Joe, and at Joe's old beat-up truck. And, 'Okay, buddy,' he said.

"He returned to his truck, raised the back section, and dumped the whole box right there on the road so that he could manoeuvre under the front of Joe's pickup. He used his hydraulic lift to raise the pickup's front end, and in about one minute had Joe's busted wheel off and the spare one on.

"Joe said he felt even more like crying, then, because he was so happy. He asked if he could pay, but the fellow told him it was nothing, that if a trucker couldn't help a buddy, especially at Christmas time, it would be a poor old world, and he told him to get on home to his family."

And it was at that point that young Julie had got up and gone. She was still in the bathroom when the Swede's powder went off at the Wilsons'. As usual, she was flushing the toilet twice, the second time by delivering a slow motion but deadly karate-style roundhouse kick to the flushing button, while washing her hands in the sink.

Her dad had told her that one day she would do damage to either the toilet or herself. The shock waves from the blast cracked the porcelain bowl in three places just as Julie delivered the karate kick, and in seconds she was up to her ankles in water, her face a freeze-frame of guilt.

Then she bellowed for help. In the living room, Samson and Jillian had jumped when the thud came, then watched, awed, as the Reverend Rawlings rose up off the ladder and seemed to glide like some great stick insect down to the sun-deck, where he landed out-spread and face up.

"That's amazing," said Jillian. "That's exactly how he landed last year."

Samson sped across the road to help the vicar, passing Sheila Martin in the hall double-timing toward the bathroom. Rawlings was rocky for a moment as Samson helped him to his feet. The vicar frowned, gingerly felt his lower back, took a few tentative steps, then slowly straightened himself up.

"Good gracious," he said. "It's gone. The kink in my back is gone." He cocked his head and looked vaguely upward. "Thank you," he said.

It took some time to convince a wailing Julie that she had not smashed the john, but it seemed likely she wouldn't be taking her feet to it for a while. When things finally settled down, the kids sat before Samson again, knees tucked up, waiting, and he resumed the story.

"Well, as I said, Joe watched the dump truck go. But there was something bugging him. Just then the two guys from the dump office came along in their car. Joe flagged them down and asked them who the guy was in the big red-and-cream dumper that had followed him out and down the road—which led only to the dump, by the way, and had no houses on that stretch."

Samson stopped to wave out the window at Svensen, who was passing with Conrad, his old German shepherd, at his heels. Svensen waved back cheerily, clearly happy with his day's doings.

"And who was it?" asked Jillian, a little snarky at the delay, and just a touch sarcastic. "One of the elves?"

Samson grinned down at them.

"I don't know," he said. "And neither did the guys from the dump. They told Joe that he had been the last one out that night, and if he had seen a big red-and-cream dump truck coming down that road then he had seen a lot more than either of them had, and they asked if he was sure he was all right."

The only sound in the living room was a small pop and crackle from the split fir in the fireplace. Samson poured himself a coffee.

Jillian gazed thoughtfully out the window, watching the Swede and Conrad in the distance. The young one stared into the dancing flames. She was rocking gently back and forth, and a small smile was working itself around the corners of her mouth.

Smoothing the Route

Jillian Martin heard about the carry-on at the Easter parade rehearsal on Good Friday when the phone call came about her younger sister, Julie. Once she learned that Julie would survive, she resumed fretting on her own problem.

She had phoned Froelich as soon as she discovered the hummingbird's nest just before lunch. The little cluster of lichen and cobwebs was the first hummer's home she had ever found. It was also sitting in a small cedar on the lot that Froelich was clearing, and she really hadn't expected any more from the Inlet grouch than what she got: "Come on, kid, eh? I got a buyer for that lot. Hummin' birds'r a dime a dozen."

While Jillian had been worrying about the hummer's immediate future, the organizers of the Easter parade in the village were watching with dismay as the wheels started falling off their practice run. There's been a parade every Easter Monday in Spinner's Inlet since anyone can remember. In recent years, the event has drawn visitors from all the other Gulf Islands and from the mainland, and Miss Bell-Atkinson, concerned for both local pride and her reputation as parade marshall, insisted on a dress rehearsal to smooth out any possible bumps.

It seems now that the event will be smooth as cream, with just one slight detour from the usual route. The run-through may be discussed for some time.

The trouble started with Lennie Wilson, in one of his egalitarian moods, insisting that his unstable billy-goat, Silas, had as much right in the parade as young Heather Spooner's beribboned horses, or Svensen's German shepherd, Conrad, who always pulls a small cart holding the Easter Bunny. It worsened with the appearance of the grey mare that Heather Spooner bought at Christmas from some farmer over on Saltspring.

Ever since Heather opened her riding stables her horses have been at the heart of the parade, pulling everything from the vicar's pre-served Model T which he doesn't like to start, to an ancient and pol-ished fire truck and a variety of traps and buggies loaded with self-declared celebrities such as Miss Bell-Atkinson. As well, there's always a squad of kids mounted proudly in pressed and polished rid-ing gear.

The horses, brushed and groomed, were standing in four files of two, with little Julie Martin up on the mare, when Lennie arrived with the goat. The mare got one whiff of the yellow-eyed buck and went for it at a dead run, lips back and teeth bared.

Young Julie shot from the saddle like a small missile, yelping as she smacked her arm against Miss Bell-Atkinson's stone gatepost, and crumpled up, howling. Dr. Timothy grabbed her and an hour later brought her back with her tears dried, her cracked left wrist hoisted proudly in plaster and sling, and traces of chocolate egg on most of her face.

In the time they were away, the mare introduced severe rifts to several relationships, and almost an end to the parade. It did also in-advertently help the older Martin girl out of her hummingbird di-lemma and made it unnecessary for her to lie down in front of Froelich's bulldozer as she had vowed to her mother she would.

During the departure of Julie Martin from her saddle, the mare continued her menacing advance on Lennie's noisome goat, which fled under the attack into Miss Bell-Atkinson's lovingly nurtured bed of late-developing daffodils. The goat nipped madly at the blooms as it ran, and the ones it didn't get were pulped under the mare's tramping hooves.

With Miss Bell-Atkinson raging at and chasing the horse, and Heather trotting after both of them, the vicar had a go at Lennie, blasting him for imposing his stinking beast on a parade of decent Christians. Lennie said that that, especially on a Good Friday, was a hell of an attitude to be taken by the Church, and the vicar promised to discuss that institution's position on the matter, in the unlikely event that Lennie were ever found within its walls.

The goat crashed bleating into the woods and the mare stopped, tossing her head and snorting triumphantly at the beast's withdrawal, in the middle of Miss Bell-Atkinson's rhubarb. Miss Bell-Atkinson tore into Heather, posing serious questions about the horse's morals, ancestry and intellect, and Heather's state of mind when she bought it.

Lennie, feeling bad for Heather, interceded and said that maybe in some small way he could share the blame. Miss Bell-Atkinson told him to shut up, and advised him that he matched his goat in everything except a sense of when to leave. Heather, on the other hand, turned on him and told him he was damned right that it was his fault, and he and his disgusting ruminant should be banned from the public highways.

The Brigadier, in an attempt to placate and resolve, went to the mare, caught up her reins, and got her halfway back before she gave him a quick nip on the bum, at which Heather couldn't help laughing and which prompted the Brigadier to observe ominously that horse-whips weren't named for nothing, and that mounts today, like certain young people, weren't all that they used to be. Heather said she was taking her horses home where they belonged and suggested the mare's unusual behaviour might be attributed to the type of company it had been put among, not including goats.

That's where events stood when Froelich rumbled by with his chainsaw and gas cans in the back. He stopped long enough to find out what had happened, and to guffaw at the mess before roaring off.

He roared almost into an enraged Lennie Wilson just around the blind bend on Borrowdale Road, where Lennie rode his bike down the yellow line, howling into the woods to an unheeding Silas. Froelich avoided tragedy only by peeling off into the bush, where his progress was interrupted by a hundred-year-old Douglas fir. A short time later, he too was in an arm cast, and had been put on light-to-no work for the next three months at least.

"Thank heavens for that," said Jillian Martin when she heard. "They'll be hatched nicely by then."

After the smoke cleared at the rehearsal, the Brigadier again took it on himself to mend fences and try to get Heather's horses back on track for the parade.

"She is not answering the phone," he reported to Miss Bell-Atkinson on Saturday morning.

"Guilt," said Miss B-A.

The Brigadier persuaded her to accompany him to the stables, where Heather met them halfway across the yard.

"Now look, Heather," the Brigadier said, "About the mare."

"She's not going in the parade," Heather said.

"But. . . . "

"Come here," Heather said, and led them over to the paddock.

A big old cherry tree was fat still with clusters of white blossom. A scattering of petals slipped away on a slight breeze and floated down to touch the mare. Some of them settled on the wide-eyed, silksoft colt that she had birthed two hours before, and which was making efforts to get onto its long, knobby legs.

"Oh, my dear!" said Miss Bell-Atkinson.

"Good show!" said the Brigadier.

"I had no idea," Heather said. "They didn't say anything when I bought her. I thought she had just got a bit fat and sassy."

The two Martin girls sat on the rail fence, eyes fixed on the foal and his mother. The young one turned briefly to her sister. "You wanna sign my cast?"

"In a minute," the older one said.

The Brigadier polled the parade committee and all agreed to slightly alter the route, so that the new arrival at Heather's stable will get a good look at what'll be expected of him next year.

Rocking the Boat

"I think we owe the man an apology," Samson Spinner said.

Lennie Wilson choked on his pint, and the table rocked. Nelson Spinner, Samson's uncle, stopped with his glass halfway to his mouth, and examined Samson.

"You got too much sun," he concluded, and sank his draft.

"And it should be a public one," Samson persisted. "What you did out there yesterday," he nodded at Lennie, "was a disgrace."

Lennie regained his speech and uttered a brisk response that had Maurice behind the Cedars bar looking over and shaking an admonishing finger, to which Lennie also had an unsubtle reply.

"That's what I mean, you see," Samson said. "That's the kind of language you used to the man . . . and you threw beer bottles."

"Only because I didn't have a gun handy," Lennie answered.

Lennie, Nelson, and Samson had been out fishing, trolling up and down about half a mile off shore of the Long Point, in Samson's old 16-footer, running quality control tests on a couple of six-packs of Nelson's home-brewed bitter as they went. At the same time they were keeping a casual watch on two of the Brannigan kids who had acquired a car-top 12-footer and a nine-horse motor and were giving them a trial run closer in to shore.

They didn't see the sloop until the Brannigan kids yelled out. The man at the helm of the big sailboat appeared to have swung deliberately in toward the kids, and when he cleared them, young Finbar was clutching the shabby aluminum side with one hand and his sister Megan with the other. Fear creased their young faces as the little craft rocked and bounced in the sloop's passage.

The voice of the helmsman, a big florid-faced fellow with a rolling waistline, boomed across to the trio as the big boat swept on: ". . . off the . . . mile—you little morons. . . . "

Lennie is not a man to beat about the bushes at any time, nor slow to respond. The look on the Brannigan kids' faces simply lent him more impetus. And while the beer bottle that accompanied Lennie's rejoinder fell short of the boat and into the unheeding trough, the words of clinically personal instruction that accompanied it struck sharply home, as evidenced by the outrage on the man's face, and the startled eyes of his single crew member.

Nelson protested when Lennie started throwing bottles at the retreating vessel—not at the act itself but on the grounds that Lennie did not have the pitching arm to actually hit either the man or the blue-trimmed white boat, and therefore was uselessly depleting Nelson's bottle stocks.

"It's the thought that counts," Lennie said, his arm back to throw another. "The gesture."

The yachtsman pointed threateningly at them and shook his fist—a mild thing compared with Lennie's own marine signals—as the yacht cut away through the greenish waters of the strait.

Samson powered over to the Brannigans' boat where Finbar was composing himself and comforting his sister. They were just getting the kids reorganized and turned around when the sloop reappeared.

Sails straining, sleek as a white shark, and as dangerous, it flashed by them only yards away and the man screamed at them clearly this time, "Get off the measured mile . . . you damned idiots!" while his sailing mate hung onto the gunwale, eyes widening as Lennie's mad cries raised dramatic speculations about the man's preferences and practices.

Lennie also scrabbled around for something to throw, but the swell from the sailboat pushed broadside into both smaller craft, starting Megan Brannigan to howling and all of them scrambling for balance while the boats danced and and dipped.

They calmed the Brannigan kids and got them headed home, and it was Nelson who then recognized the issue.

"That old arbutus there." He pointed to the great leaning, barkless tree anchored on a headland of rock to the east. "And the bell buoy. The sailing types out of Vancouver used to use that as their measured mile for testing their new boats. I guess they've started doing it again. We were in the way of his test run." And he added, "You recognize him now, don't you?"

They did. The man was Lloyd Cardew-Holt, a life insurance salesman from the mainland who with his wife had recently bought five acres on Oyster Bay and built, for weekend use, a garish, seven-bedroom affair of concrete and glass whose only submission to good taste was that it couldn't be seen from the road because of a fortuitously placed stand of fir.

His wife, acquired within the last couple of years, is a lady a good many years his senior whose holdings include Florida and Caribbean real estate, and the family purse strings. Supervising the completion of their waterfront love nest from behind pitchers of Tanqueray martinis had exhausted her and she was taking her recovery in a three-week retreat at a fat farm near San Diego.

In Lennie's opinion the man's hyphenated surname made him a poseur, his job made him a charlatan, and his taste in architecture, an oaf. Given all of this, Lennie was incensed when Samson continued to insist that an apology for the bottle tossing was in order. He finally declared Samson had gone soft in the head, finished his drink, and stalked out of the Cedars muttering about the erosion of character, integrity, and spine.

And if he was angry then, he was perfectly fit to be locked up when Samson actually did go public with the apology—right in the middle of the letters page in *The Tidal Times*. Elliott Smalley was so impressed with the tone that he placed it in a six-point box and headed it: A Gracious Statement. The clipping was pinned up and framed on the notice boards outside Logan's store, the community hall, and the Legion.

"My arse," Lennie fumed, stabbing at the headline as he spread the paper out on the table in the Cedars and glared at Samson with a mixture of anger and confusion. "And how the hell come you think you can speak for me and Nelson . . . ?"

He glared also at Nelson, who shrugged, stood up and strolled to the bar to get a pickled egg.

"Have you read it?" Samson asked, sitting comfortably back with a glass of dark ale.

"I've read the bloody headline, and seen my name at the bottom—'Have I read it?' " he repeated, dripping scorn.

Nelson Spinner sauntered back from the bar, took his seat with his feet up, bit into the egg and washed it down with about half the mug of draft. He grinned at Lennie.

Lennie looked at the pair of them. Samson smiled at him. Lennie studied him for a second, then he leaned over and started reading. " 'And for our unforgiveable behaviour' . . . unforgiveable! Bollocks!"

"Well, you *were* quite rude," Samson said, as Lennie started sputtering.

Lennie shook his head, then carried on.

" 'And so we offer our humble' . . . —humble!—Jesus!—' . . . humble apologies to Mr. Cardew-Holt . . . and to his lovely young companion, the lady in the unique single-strand pink string bikini, with the glorious summer tan. Her obvious youth and innocence should not have been exposed to the kind of language that sullied the air that fine afternoon. . . . ' " Lennie stopped reading and aimed a quizzical eye at Nelson, who invited him to read on.

" 'To that young woman, who we have learned usually carries out important professional and secretarial duties for Mr. Cardew-Holt in his mainland office. . . . ' "

Lennie stopped. Then he cackled.

"Oh, you dirty bugger," he said, his head shaking in undisguised admiration.

"Thank you," Nelson accepted the compliment.

"And Mrs. Cardew-Holt. . . ?"

"Is due back on this afternoon's ferry, I believe," Samson said.

Elliott Smalley said it was very kind of Lennie to help him with his weekly chore of handing out copies of the *Times* to all vehicles unloading from the *Gulf Queen*.

"It's my great pleasure, Elliott," Lennie said. "Believe me."

All of a Lather

The Martin girls swapped looks and got up from the table.

"And I mean *plenty* of soap," Grandma Tyson said. "I can smell him from here."

Young Julie opened her mouth to answer, but Jillian grabbed her and bundled her out of the living room. "Don't start arguing again," she said. "She'll tell dad, and then *they'll* be at it. Let's stick him in the bath and get it over with."

The girls' grandmother was halfway through her annual two-month visit from England and, as always, was setting things straight. The Martins generally dearly love Grandma Tyson, but, as Sheila Martin (*née* Tyson) has been heard to say, if there is any one occasion in the year they look forward to more than her mother's arrival, it is the old lady's departure when the stay is over.

"Just to get that ten-month breather," Sheila says.

Paul Martin has often been much more succinct about his mother-in-law's penchant for rearranging his home.

Julie expressed the situation from her point of view to one of her Brannigan family associates: "She kisses me half to death for the first week, but then she gets kinda bossy and an' makes up all sortsa new rules 'n stuff."

Such as the order to sanitize Charlie. "The dog stinks," Grandma had said earlier. "Put him outside, where dogs are meant to be."

"No!" Julie's rejection of that notion was loud and from the heart. Julie had never doubted the superiority of dumb creatures over man, and the appearance of Charlie six months ago simply cemented her convictions.

He was about three months old then, abandoned by a tourist family, a black bag of bones with a white shirt-front, discovered by Julie as he stood shivering, half-starved, and staring optimistically up at the Martins' house from the bottom of the driveway.

He has since evolved into a recognizable and perky, if somewhat short, springer spaniel, with an intelligent eye and a developed sense of survival. On Grandma Tyson's arrival he displayed an immediate, and wholly justified, apprehension.

She very quickly relieved Charlie of his claim on the old rocker by the woodstove, and moved his wicker basket as close to the back door as was possible without being on the porch. Paul Martin bore the changes as he does every year, with a visible fortitude.

Grandma Tyson's suggestion that Charlie be banished to the outdoors horrified Julie.

"He would catch a cold an' would be lonely an'—" she cast around for the direst of fates "—things would get him!"

She also opposed her grandmother's remarks concerning Charlie's fragrance. "That's just... dog... for heaven's sake. Dogs always smell different from people." And after a moment she added, "In fact Charlie smells better than a lot of people." Which drew a sharp look over her grandmother's glasses.

Julie had reluctantly agreed to a compromise bath for Charlie who, even though Jillian casually spelled out the B word while ostensibly examining a pack of forbidding rain clouds out the window, almost made it to the basement stairs before being collared and bum-slid across the bathroom floor to the tub.

Grandma Tyson came in twice during the festivities and each time insisted on more shampoo. "Get the dandruff and everything," she said.

"We'll wash him *white* if we use any more," Julie argued, but Jillian signalled her for peace, and poured on more shampoo. They were halfway through that rinse when Grandma Tyson came in again.

"He still smells," she said. She took the shampoo bottle, unscrewed the cap, and poured the lot over Charlie's neck and shoulders. "That should do it," she said.

It did. Charlie's tolerance was breached. He slipped through Jillian's hands, scrambled over the edge of the tub, shot between Grandma Tyson's legs, and was out the back door, off the porch, and legging it down the driveway without a backward look.

"Now look what you've done!" Julie yelled, and went after him, paying no attention to the rain that had started seconds ago and was now falling in torrents.

Paul Martin was half a mile away in his pickup, heading home, and musing on his relationship with his mother-in-law. It was vastly improved from the early days, but could still occasionally be tense.

Paul had met Sheila Tyson when, as a young man looking for a challenge he finished up in the Third Battalion of the British army's Parachute Regiment. While tracking down members of the Spinner clan, he had asked Sheila for directions in the Cumbrian coast town of Whitehaven, and it went from there. Grandma Tyson considered him a dubious choice, given the usually well-earned reputation of the young men who wear the red beret and the parachutist's blue and white wings. The fact that he intended to remove her daughter 7,000 miles to the other side of Canada was confirmation of most of her suspicions.

Her views mellowed after they persuaded her to make her first trip, and especially following the birth of her two grand-daughters, on whom she dotes—although they occasionally need sorting out.

Paul has accepted a truce. He still becomes rattled when she insists on reordering his home, and frequently starches the atmosphere by saying so. He was already close to his limit over the business with Charlie. He entertained these thoughts as he swung around the corner on the bottom road, and jammed on his brakes at the sight of the apparition straddling the centre line. He would later say it looked like an explosion in a soap factory.

It was Charlie, broken out into a fine full lather from the combined effects of the excess of shampoo, the pouring rain, and his own exertions. His eyes blinked from deep inside a cloud of foam and his tongue flopped like a small pink flag.

But there was more to come than just Charlie and suds. In braking as abruptly as he did, Paul seriously disadvantaged the Brigadier who had been peering through the windshield of his Mini-minor and using Paul's tail lights as a guide through the rainstorm. The Brigadier clipped and extinguished the left-side light as he veered away from Paul's pickup and into the path of the Reverend Randall Rawlings coming the other way in his old Volvo. The vicar braked, hydroplaned a few feet, and halted sharply with his front bumper embedded in the Mini's door.

There followed a series of angry exchanges in which the Brigadier challenged Paul's right to stop just when he felt like it, Paul questioned the Brigadier's competence to be driving anything bigger than a grocery cart, and the vicar described the situation in terms that, if it hadn't been for the rain slamming down on them, could clearly have sounded less than suitable for a man of the cloth.

Charlie was so glad to see anyone not waving a shampoo container that he leapt at all three in turn, spraying them with thick flecks of lather.

Paul left the vicar and the Brigadier yelling at each other through the downpour. He stuck Charlie on the floor and ordered him to stay down. A hundred yards down the road he stopped for a sodden, sobbing Julie, who fell on Charlie and kissed him, deaf to her father's questions, all the way back to the house.

Out of the truck, and furious, Paul demanded to know immediately who was responsible for the lunacy that had embarrassed him and caused God knows how many hundreds of dollars worth of damage to three vehicles.

The two girls stood on the porch, looking from each other to Charlie, who puzzled at the off-white puddles sudsing around his oversized feet. Grandma Tyson hovered behind the screen door, a small alarm showing in her face.

"Well?" Paul demanded.

Julie turned toward the screen door. She opened her mouth.

"We did!" Jillian spoke. "We did. We were fooling around."

Paul looked at each of them. Julie's eyes pointed to her shoes. He looked toward the screen door.

"Right," he said. "You will formally apologise to the vicar and to the Brigadier." Julie groaned. Jillian rolled her eyes. "And you lose a month's allowance."

Julie's eyes flamed and she cried, "That's no fair . . . !" but her sister yanked her away and talked intently into her ear. Julie kicked the porch, glanced at the screen door, and subsided.

When Sheila Martin arrived home she was surprised to see her mother brushing and holding a jolly conversation with a gleaming Charlie, who, while cocking a suspicious eye at Grandma Tyson, gratefully accepted the treats she insisted on shovelling into him.

For kids without an allowance the Martin girls continued remarkably well-supplied with such of life's staples as Mars bars, Archie comics, and all the Sweet Valley High books they could handle.

Bargain Day

Samson Spinner watched buyers carting away the last of the items from the rummage sale, and he accepted the vicar's sincere thanks and congratulations.

"People always come through if you have the faith," the Reverend Randall Rawlings smiled. "Even the ones you might least expect to."

"He was right, too," Samson conceded to his uncle, Nelson, over a Sunday-brunch pint in the Cedars the next day. "Until I got to Froelich's place on Friday I was thinking they might as well cancel the sale," he said.

Samson had been doing his bit during the week for the Church in the Vale, in lieu of attendance, by collecting for the Saturday rummage sale. By late Friday he was impressed neither with the receptions he'd met nor with the stuff in his pickup, much of which, if his memory was any good at all, he recognized as unsaleable junk that had been left over at last year's sale.

When he called at Miss Bell-Atkinson's place she stood behind the curtain and pointed imperiously to a cardboard box on the porch. While Miss Bell-Atkinson is a pillar of the Church, and all in favour of yarding beer drinkers and other sinners into the fold, when it comes to actually coughing up, she has the pockets of a Scottish banker. The box held four plastic cups with faded Ronald McDonald logos, and two lampshades made in Taiwan apparently long before that republic's insistence on some form of quality control.

Lennie Wilson, who last week failed to win the vicar's support for his argument that if Jesus turned water into wine there is no good reason why Lennie should not be able to turn it into grain alcohol, grudgingly donated a garden rake with four teeth missing. At Samson's next stop, Svensen claimed the rake was one Lennie had borrowed from him two years ago, and he took it, went inside, and shut the door.

Chief Jimmy Plummer agreed that he had promised to donate a

cord of split alder. He also said he'd been too busy to split it, or for that matter to fall the trees, but that Samson could borrow his chainsaw and maul, provided he used his own gas.

The only ones home at the Martin house were Julie and Jillian. They said Samson could have a pair of slippers that their grandma had left behind when she returned to England. On examination it was clear that Charlie the spaniel had done a close investigation of the slippers, and Samson declined the offer. Julie said she was sure her grandma's slippers were as good as any of the rubbish that was bound to be for sale, and said if he wanted to change his mind she herself would wipe all the dog spit off them.

Samson parked outside Sebastian's place and pretended not to see two of the Brannigan boys, Mick and Rory, going through the pile of items in the pickup as he climbed the Whittles' steps. Nor was he suprised when the pair of them walked away empty-handed.

Sebastian gave him a whole box of crisp, fresh, untouched, last year's Gulf Islands ferry schedules. When Samson asked him what sort of use he saw the schedules being put to, Sebastian became quite snappish and said that if more people recognized a giving nature when they saw one, the world wouldn't have half the problems it does.

At *The Tidal Times*, Elliott Smalley offered a coupon for two free ads for anyone buying a year's subscription to the paper. Samson pointed out that Elliott already gives four free ads with a subscription. Elliott said it was all a matter of newspaper logistics that the average person didn't understand and that he didn't have time to explain, and he went back to editing copy and asked Samson to close the door after himself.

"Then I get to Froelich's," he told Nelson, shaking his head.

He had not expected anything better than a rude dismissal at the home of the Inlet misanthrope. As it was, the Froelichs weren't home.

"Probably embarrassed by his own generosity," Samson told Nelson.

Samson had been about to get back in the truck when he saw the cardboard sign leaning against the house: "Sale stuff in the shed" and an arrow pointing to Froelich's workshop.

Samson almost regretted everything he'd called Froelich, when he saw the stuff piled up neatly waiting to be moved. There were brass fireplace fenders from decades ago, several mahogany-veneer small tables, vases and other pottery, a roll-top desk, candlesticks . . . and on. Samson brought the truck back three times before he got it all moved.

"I guess people just mellow as they get older," Samson said. "The vicar says he's never seen stuff move so fast, nor so much money come in in one day."

They finished their pints and Samson declined another on the grounds he might take up Chief Jimmy's offer on the alder. "Be ready for next year, anyway," he said.

He was flagged down by a stranger as he passed Froelich's place. Samson confirmed for the man that it was indeed the Froelich residence. The man frowned.

"That's funny. He said he had left all the items in his shed, but I don't see anything. Is there another shed, do you know?"

"Items?" Samson said.

The man explained that he owned an antique store in Victoria, had negotiated the purchase of a load of furnishings that had come to Froelich from the estate of a relative, and was supposed to pick it all up today while Froelich was in Seattle for the weekend.

The man gestured to his van parked by the house. "I'm going to have to make the damned trip over again," he said. "What a screw up, eh?"

Samson said that certainly did seem to sum things up.

Don Hunter is a teacher turned journalist, TV script-writer and author. A long-time reporter for *The Province,* in Vancouver, he is the author of *Sasquatch* and of the CBC-TV movie and series "9B". Don and his wife, June, came to Canada from England in 1961; they and their two daughters live in Richmond, BC, and also have a home in the Gulf Islands.

"Hunter has lined up the quintessential quirks and quarks, the qualities, the eccentricities, the toughness, loyalty, courage and independence of the Gulf Islanders . . . the wry humour and sly ways . . . he's been there."   *Barry Broadfoot, author*